SUMMER LOVIN'

First published 2013 by
FREMANTLE PRESS
25 Quarry Street, Fremantle 6160
(PO Box 158, North Fremantle 6159)
Western Australia
www.fremantlepress.com.au

Editor Naama Amram
Designer Allyson Crimp
Cover images by cdwheatley (beach) and clintscholz (sky) — iStockphoto.com
Printed by Everbest Printing Company, China

National Library of Australia
Cataloguing-in-Publication entry

Title: Summer lovin' / Introduction by Liz Byrski.
ISBN: 9781922089588 (paperback)
Other Authors/Contributors: Byrski, Liz.
Dewey Number: A823.01

Government of **Western Australia**
Department of **Culture and the Arts**

Fremantle Press is supported by the State Government through the
Department of Culture and the Arts.

SUMMER LOVIN'

INTRODUCTION *by* LIZ BYRSKI

Stories by

JOAN LONDON ★ CRAIG SILVEY
A.B. FACEY ✦ ELIZABETH JOLLEY
NATASHA LESTER ☀ MARCELLA POLAIN
CHRIS MCLEOD ⚓ JACQUELINE WRIGHT
and more

FREMANTLE PRESS
fine independent publishing

CONTENTS

INTRODUCTION

Only connect! That was the whole of her sermon. Only connect the prose and the passion, and both will be exalted, and human love will be seen at its height. Live in fragments no longer.

E.M. Forster
Howards End

How does one begin to write about love? It ought to be easy but try to pin love down in words on a page and it becomes elusive, unruly and clichéd. We feel love, yearn for it, recognise it when we see it, celebrate its gifts, fear and grieve for its loss, bathe in its light and struggle when its withdrawal plunges us into darkness. We know that it can transcend age, sex, race, faith and distance, but that it doesn't always fulfil its promise; happy ever after can turn to bitterness if it is infected with suspicion, betrayal and boredom. And yet we still believe in it.

'Whatever in love means,' said Prince Charles when, on the day of his engagement to Lady Diana Spencer, he was asked if he were in love. His answer drew a sharp intake of breath from romantics around the world; it wasn't what we'd wanted to hear. Charles may never have been the ideal model of Prince Charming but he was the world's most eligible bachelor and we needed him to confirm the magic of that fairytale romance. And so we rolled our eyes and spoke of awkwardness, inadequacy, of the need of the royals to get their act together, and we thanked our gods for Diana and what she might bring to a family hidebound by duty, formality and convention and so apparently emotionally inadequate.

Fortunately for most of us our own failures at the hands of love do not have to be lived out in the public spotlight. From the comfort and safety of our armchairs we can become expert critics. But whether we gasped or griped at the Prince's words on that engagement day, he was asking the question that we all face at some time in our lives — what *does* it mean to be in love? What *does* love mean? And what can we learn when, in any of its forms, love goes wrong? Love eludes logic and confounds analysis, it taunts and teases us, rewards and punishes and yet we continue to reach for it because love, in all its infinite varieties, is at the heart of life, and if life matters then so, inevitably, does love.

Through the stories in this collection, some of Western Australia's best known and admired writers get to grips with life's most precious and unruly emotion. These stories take us from teenage confusion to effortless sensuality, and from the lifelong love of family and friends and place to the shadows of ignorance and deception that can so easily make fools of us. We visit the barren waste of lovelessness and the power of memory that can make love and the lover feel reborn.

In Jacqueline Wright's opening piece, 'But Slowly', Annie longs for Mick but also for acceptance by the Indigenous people with whom she is to work. With great subtlety Wright lets us feel the trust that has built love in that community, its magnetic force and Annie's yearning to become a part of it through her feelings for Mick. *Make haste slowly*, he warns her, *More slowly than you could ever imagine.* It's sound advice but love rarely adapts to slowing down, and the urgency is even greater in youth. For the lonely Saul, in Adam Morris's 'Rental', nothing moves fast enough. He has found a place of his own which allows his dreams of love to flourish, but when they fail to materialise the only thing that heads towards him at great pace is bitter disappointment.

Eleanor Rigby, in Craig Silvey's 'Chellow', doesn't do slow, nor does she waste time on niceties; music and curiosity propel her towards a chance at love. She is brave and bold in confronting Ewan and her blindness saves her from the fear and confusion she might otherwise have detected in his face. Fear and confusion also haunt Annabel Smith's teenage protagonist in 'Delta'. Charlie is caught in the wash of his twin brother's amorous escapades and, aching for experiment and discovery, he falls into the oldest of love traps. In 'New', Hovsanna, a young bride, is bewildered by that which takes place every night in the bedroom. Bound by the ignorance of sex so long deemed appropriate for young women and girls, Hovsanna consults her mother-in-law, and Marcella Polain creates a tender and subtle connection between two very different women.

The rapture and intensity of falling in love are exquisitely captured by Tracy Farr, who holds us in the magic of that heightened sensuality in which the swish of silk against skin and a simple glance or gesture take on a powerful meaning. As Lena and Beatrix cross Sydney Harbour on the Manly Ferry, as they light their cigarettes and study the paintings in Beatrix's studio, love, desire and art come together to 'Trick the Light'. That same sense of rapture is alive in Natasha Lester's 'Just Like the Heart', only here it pulsates more slowly as Alix, a heart surgeon, and Dan, a sculptor of bodies and body parts, begin to know each other. *What does it feel like to touch a heart that is still working?* Dan asks, and Alix realises for the first time that it is a feeling akin to love.

Love's tangled webs though can bring all sorts of failures, and Harry and Carole in Iris Lavell's 'Under the Circumstances' remind us with wry humour how swiftly and easily the thrilling promise of illicit sex can end in awkwardness and humiliation. Meanwhile, Tim, the narrator of Chris McLeod's 'The Wedding Suit', studies his wife's back as he contemplates how and when he will leave her and their daughter to live with the lover who is pressing him to act. There is nothing left of what they once had except love for the child, and the decision tortures him.

So often the true appreciation of love lives in reflection. A.B. Facey's 'More than Just Me' recalls a life that spanned two world wars and produced seven children. The lasting love shared for fifty-nine years with his wife, Evelyn, *the loveliest and most beautiful woman*, shines out from the core of his *fortunate life* rendering it *something which was more than just me*. Facey's story, told in such simple language, also speaks of the love of children and family, of the places we call home and the love of country. It is that great embrace of love that also inspires Lesley Corbett's 'River Fever', in which she contextualises so many forms of love within the dramatic and changing landscape of the Kimberley.

Perhaps more than any other, Elizabeth Jolley's story, 'Mr Parker's Valentine', is a reminder that it is love that puts us in touch with our humanity, and that without it we are less than human. Mr Parker is a man who has known love, and still lives it in his connection with others. Love also lives in the generous spirit of Eleanor Page, but her husband, Pearson, is caught up in the impatience and selfishness of ownership and control. It's an entrapment that has dire consequences.

British novelist Doris Lessing suggests that memory and reflection bring us the advantage of changing views. They are, she says, like a path that winds up a mountain and whenever you look back you may see a different landscape. And so it is with love. In 'Enough Rope' Joan London's narrator steals some time out to visit an old friend and struggles in the tension between past and present. There is a hopeless sort of yearning here for something now too fraught and risky to rouse — and yet there is always hope. Memory also drives my own 'Thirty-seven Years', a true story of a second chance at first love, in which memory and imagination combine to create the sense of youth recaptured, but also shed new and challenging light on past and present.

Only connect! writes E.M. Forster, and that familiar quote from *Howards End* is a potent reminder that it is the love within us that connects us to others in so many different ways. Love is the heart and the engine of our humanity: without the will to give it and to receive it we are simply less than human.

Liz Byrski
June 2013

JACQUELINE WRIGHT
BUT SLOWLY

She jumps when Mick wakes her. Moonlight marks the slim leaves of the paperbark with its liquid light. 'How long ...? Why didn't you ...?'

Mick points to the sky. A crescent moon is shining above her and she instantly thinks of Nundi's smile. 'A Nundi moon,' she says sitting up.

Mick sits up, links his fingers together and stretches them above his head. His life at Yindi has sculptured his muscles into something that looks great in faded jeans and a cotton t-shirt riddled with holes. She stretches, feigning stiffness in her limbs in order to hide the desire that radiates through her. If Mick had it his way, he would have been driving to Yindi the following day, but he has been lumped with the task of getting a budget together for an ablution block to be built for the Yindi school.

'I can organise a lift out with Noddy on the mail plane for you,' he suggests.

'I'm happy to wait until you're ready to go,' Annie says and his instant smile counters any suspicions she's been harbouring about Mick not really wanting her to come back.

So Annie puts a check on her enthusiasm and concentrates on getting through the ferocious heat, one day at a time. She attempts to ease his work burden a little by taking on odd jobs. This invariably requires her to drive from Eight Mile to town on a regular basis. The many stops along the way help her to acquaint herself with this 'corker of a town', as it is flagged on the sign. For the life of her, she can't work out what the connection between Ransom and cork is exactly. Neither, it seems, can anyone else she asks, even the woman at the Historical Society. Each time she drives past the sign it seems to lose a letter, so that soon, all that is left of the phrase on the big hunk of ore is 'a town' with the lower-case letter 'a' swinging upside down. She discovers that the bar at the roadhouse between the old and new parts of town makes phenomenal barramundi burgers. She gets to know the cook's wife quite well. Elsie reminds her a little of her Aunty Ellen. She oozes with small-town friendliness, but not in an overbearing kind of way. She provides Annie with useful tips on bait and specials going on biscuits at the supermarket.

At Eight Mile, Mick and Annie resume their ritual, eating together and sitting outside of an evening, enjoying the breeze, which takes a clean swipe at the heated land. Annie's taken to filling paper bags with sand and placing candles inside them. Instead of discussing her past, Annie chats about her day. She finds out that the camp she explored belonged to someone who had died. That raking or sweeping of the earth obliterates the dead person's footprints so that their spirit will not remain attached to familiar places and they can live in peace in the spirit world. That the wailing at the ceremony was the grieving of the mothers and the skin mothers of the death of the initiates' boyhood. Annie tells Mick about what she learns from what he calls the 'hysterical society'. The creation of Ransom by some knobbly-kneed prospector who discovered manganese and sold his lease to a multinational mining company for a carton of beer and a windmill. Occasionally, Mick volunteers snippets from the office: how Tommy got his car stolen, a break-in at the school. The dodgy antics of Smithie, the new purchasing officer, begin to feature a little more regularly. Mick tells Annie about Smithie's propensity to dish dirt any chance he gets.

'He's also an atrocious judge of character. That's why we get dickhead builders who charge three times as much, take twice as long to finish anything. Then we've got to hire someone else to come and fix their mistakes.'

Mick refers to Smithie as 'the dirty little dobber', and Annie's prepared to accept this bad character record at face value because Mick rarely passes judgement on anyone.

They watch the dramatic display of lightning lacing the horizon.

'Why have they stopped burning tyres?'

'Law Business has finished now so it can rain as much as it likes.'

'If black smoke keeps rain away, what brings it?' Annie sits up.

'Good smells.'

'Like incense?'

He laughs. 'Tasty cooking smells, like meat.'

Annie makes a mental note: Buy yummy sausages from the halal section of the supermarket.

She announces proudly that she's worked out there are three types of spinifex.

'Only three, hey?'

When the breeze gets strong enough to blow the bags onto the flame of the candles and set them on fire, Mick says he's going to bed. While she waits for him to finish his shower, she listens to cars grumbling around like old tomcats, fights breaking out between dogs, and the cows bellowing and stomping around in search of water.

One day, when Annie delivers a car part to Mick at the Eight Mile office, she finds Tommy Mutton there talking into the microphone of a reel-to-reel tape recorder. He is sitting with a silver-whiskered, silver-haired man with the dictionary she saw when she first arrived at Eight Mile. She squeezes herself into a corner, pretends to sort through papers while listening to their gruff mumblings.

'Story number twenty,' the other man says heavily, adjusting the spectacles on his nose. He waves at Tommy. Tommy holds one of his drawings about two inches from his nose and squints at it. He begins talking, all in language. The other man listens, occasionally interjecting, to tell him sharply, 'Speak up!' Tommy pauses and then starts again, louder and more laboured in his speech.

'Jipi,' he says when he has finished.

Annie is filled with a curious mixture of admiration and envy. That evening, she asks Mick how she can possibly make Tommy talk to her in the same way.

'Learn the language,' he laughs, and when Annie doesn't join in he mumbles, 'There's lots of layers of oppression, Annie. Too many for one person to dig through in a little under three months.'

'I know you think what I'm doing is grandiose but how else will Tommy's voice be heard? The UN's role is to advocate for those who do not have a strong enough voice of their own.'

Encouraged by the tilt of his head, she continues. 'The philosophy driving the UN is that human beings have dignity, human life is inviolable and that people should be treated as ends in themselves, never as the means to an end. You can't argue with that.'

'It's not what you're doing that's the problem here, Annie,' Mick says gently, 'it's how you're going about it.'

She thinks of Tommy, relaxed and telling his

stories in the office today, and raises the possibility of recording the stories of the Yindi artists at the art centre.

'Make haste slowly,' says Mick, blowing out the candles. 'More slowly than you could ever imagine. Perhaps get Ruthie on side. With her help you can start to learn your standing with people and what you can and can't talk to them about.' He squeezes her hand lightly before ambling back along the verandah and inside.

That Mick forgets to mention they're travelling to Yindi the following day doesn't perturb Annie. She wakes in the morning to the sound of him singing gospel songs outside her window and knows instinctively they will be leaving. She watches him from her ritual position on the step as he finishes tying down the load. Mick's to-ing and fro-ing from donga to truck has ground the bougainvillea blooms, glued to the pavers by eucalyptus sap, to a fine powder. It spirals in soft, lazy eddies and is taken out into the desert by the last whisker of a morning breeze.

Louisa comes to Yindi with them, as do Ruthie, Kuj and the twins, Tommy Mutton, Ted and his roly-poly dog. Once on the highway, Annie fiddles around with the car cassette player, trying to get the right volume for an oral history tape she has bought from the hysterical society. When she looks up, a garbage truck on their side of the road is barrelling straight towards them. Annie screams as, at the last possible moment, the truck swerves to the other side of the road and Annie catches a glimpse of a man with long dreadlocks and tattoos all the way up his arm. Mick waves and beeps.

'Who was that idiot?' Annie finally asks when her heart slows.

'Maggot,' says Mick. 'He's the town's garbo. If the donga's not vacant, I usually camp out at his place in town.'

'He could have killed us!'

Mick laughs. 'Not Maggot.'

They ride the dusty corrugations and come to a stop at a river crossing which Ruthie calls 'Yindi Landing'.

As soon as they are out of the car, the women start fishing; short lines attached to green switches, no sinkers, flicking out fish after fish onto the bank. Small sardine-sized fish with yellowish stripes. Ruthie throws a pebble into the water before wetting the line. The splash brings the fish to the surface. The children run around collecting the fish and putting them into the soak they dig in the wet sand by the river's edge. Ted leaves his dog panting in the shallows and walks up out of the riverbed with a rifle over his shoulder. Mick brews up a strong pot of coffee on the fire and they share a tin of peaches.

When the day cools, Annie walks upstream with the children. They show her some greenish-yellow fruit the size of a small plum and tell her they are bush tomatoes, but stop her from biting into one.

'You have to take the black seeds out first,' says Kuj, wiping the fruit with the hem of her skirt.

They walk further in search of a bush fruit they call 'jima'. Jima are like blueberries only smaller. They collect only a handful. Kuj tells her that there will be plenty at the end of coldtime when the sea breeze is blowing from the west, but only if they get to them before the emus.

She spots some tussocks of grass which bear a strong likeness to Kuj's hair. She immediately regrets pointing this out to the children. One of the twins (she fails to identify which one) pulls out a clump and parades around with it on his head. Kuj stops this performance with a blast of words which Annie doesn't understand but interprets immediately as swearing. She takes Kuj's hand and guides her to the river. When Annie wades into the river for a dip, Kuj pulls her away.

'Not here,' she says, telling her about the big snake living in that particular waterhole. She shows her tracks of animals in the river mud, naming them in language, ridiculing her attempts to pronounce the words.

When they get back, emu feathers are flying everywhere. Annie takes note of a blazing fire. 'I guess we're going to stay the night,' she says to Mick who is feeding the fire.

'You guessed right,' he says, pulling a few emu feathers from her hair.

Her sleep is marked by the dog's general restlessness, the whine of mosquitoes and the rise and fall of the half-moon and Orion's Belt. Her slapping of mosquitoes is replaced by the swatting of flies as soon as the sun rises. Annie listens to the sound of Tommy singing deep and low. When she pulls herself out of the swag, she sees Mick crouching next to the dog, patting her tummy and saying how her bull-catching days are over for a while. Six pups wriggle around her legs. The bitch bares her teeth at Annie who, Mick suggests, is a bit too quick in her enthusiasm.

They eat goanna for lunch and Ruthie cooks up a damper. Louisa unearths a piece of fat from the blacked bones and skin. She hands it to Annie who holds it gingerly between her fingers. It is yellowish brown.

'Good medicine,' says Louisa, 'stops you getting sick.'

Annie shuts her eyes and swallows it whole.

'She must like it!' Ruthie tells Louisa who hands some more to Annie.

The women burst into peals of laughter when they see Annie's horrified expression.

They leave for Yindi in the cool of the afternoon. Annie is wedged between Mick and Ted who nurses one of the twins and a rifle in his lap. The pups and their mother sit by his feet. A combination of a day in the sun and her restless night has exhausted Annie. Her head rolls around and comes to rest on Mick's shoulder. She awakens to soft kissing noises as he draws on the rollie glued to his lips.

Although her eyes are still closed, Mick says softly, 'How you going there?'

She murmurs and nuzzles closer. She keeps her

head where it is until they accelerate out of the catchment and into the desert proper.

Annie notices some broad-leafed trees with thick bark. Ted names them in language and Mick tells her that CD reckons they are what is left of an old remnant rainforest. When they are less than an hour from home, Ted asks Mick to stop and he sets a few clumps of spinifex alight.

'Let people know we're coming,' answers Mick, before she gets the chance to ask. 'You can also send up a smoke to let people know you're in trouble.'

'How do they know which is which?'

'If you don't show up, then you must be in trouble.'

It's dark by the time they get home. Mick shows Annie how to pickle fish and make a green pawpaw salad. She watches him put the fish Nundi has given him into a bowl, dressing it with coconut milk, lime juice, fish sauce, chopped coriander, spring onions and chilli.

Annie fiddles with the tuning button of the long-range radio. The best she can come up with is Frank Sinatra crooning 'A Foggy Day in London Town'.

'My father's favourite,' she laughs, then cries out in disappointment when the crooner's voice gradually fades into a gentle hiss. Mick moves to adjust the aerial. She can feel his thigh caress her arm as he tries moving the wire around to no avail. She watches him concentrate, running his tongue over his top lip.

He catches her watching him. 'What now?' he asks.

'Never mind,' she says, unable to shift her gaze or even move away.

'Tell me,' he murmurs, running his fingers as best he can through her knotted hair and cupping the back of her skull in his hand.

(From *Red Dirt Talking*, a novel, 2012.)

A.B. FACEY
MORE THAN JUST ME

On May twenty-fifth something happened that shocked all who saw it. Quite a few of us were sitting on the edge of our dugouts watching the navy ships shelling the Turkish positions away beyond our frontline. One large ship, the *Triumph*, was sending shells over our position from what seemed about two miles off shore. Suddenly there was a terrible explosion and for a few seconds we wondered what had happened. Then we realised that the *Triumph* had been hit by a torpedo. She started to list to the side and within fifteen minutes was completely upside down with her two propellers out of the water. In another half an hour she had disappeared completely. After the torpedo struck, the guns, both fore and aft, were firing as fast as they could and those gunners must have gone down with their ship. We considered this one of the most gallant acts of bravery that we had seen and we had seen many by this time. Most of the crew jumped overboard, and destroyers and small boats went to their rescue. We were told that about four hundred had lost their lives.

A few days after the armistice we received some trench comfort parcels from home. Everything was very quiet this day, and a sergeant-major and several men with bags of parcels came along our line and threw each of us a parcel. I got a pair of socks in my parcel. Having big feet — I take a ten in boots — I called out to my mates saying that I had a pair of socks that I would be glad to swap for a bigger pair as I didn't think they would fit. Strange as it seems, I was the only person in my section to get socks; the others got all kinds of things such as scarves, balaclavas, vests, notepaper, pencils, envelopes and handkerchiefs. I found a note rolled up in my socks and it read: 'We wish the soldier that gets this parcel the best of luck and health and a safe return home to his loved ones when the war is over.' It was signed, 'Evelyn Gibson, Hon. Secretary, Girl Guides, Bunbury, W.A.' A lot of my mates came from Bunbury so I asked if any of them knew an Evelyn Gibson. They all knew her and said that she was a good-looker and very smart, and that she came from a well-liked and respected family. I told them that she was mine and we all had an argument, in fun, about this girl and we all claimed her.

The socks, when I tried them on, fitted perfectly and they were hand-knitted with wool. That was the only parcel I received while at Gallipoli.

Not long after delivering the prisoners and returning back to my unit, my part in the campaign ended. While I was on look-out duty, a shell lobbed into the parapet of our trench and exploded, killing my mate. Several bags filled with sand were blown on top of me — this hurt me badly inside and crushed my right leg. I had difficulty walking or standing upright, and then, while moving to the tunnel to go through to the doctor, a bullet hit me in the shoulder.

The doctor examined me and ordered me to be taken away. At the dressing-station I was bandaged and sent on to the main clearing-station at Headquarters. From there I was to be put on a hospital ship anchored about one mile off shore.

We arrived at Fremantle near the end of November 1915, after a very rough trip. I was very ill and still vomiting blood and getting those nasty fainting feelings; the doctor on the ship had kept me in bed. I felt as if there was something amiss deep down inside. I had had this feeling ever since I was wounded. The hospitals in Egypt had given me all sorts of treatment and medicines, including hot and cold packs and massages — these remedies gave me severe pain so they stopped them.

On arriving at Fremantle, about one hundred of us

were taken straight to the No. 8 Australian Military Hospital at Fremantle. From there I got twenty-four hours to leave and was allowed to go home to my stepfather's place in West Perth. My relations and friends were all pleased to see me home again.

When I reported back to hospital the next morning I was ordered to bed and there I remained until Christmas time. Many doctors and specialists examined me but none of them were sure what was wrong — my wounds had all healed. I was put through all sorts of tests.

One day while on leave, I went to Perth with another soldier from the hospital (these daily leaves were from eleven a.m. to eleven p.m.). We were walking down Barrack Street in a northerly direction when we saw two girls coming towards us. We were in uniform and had our battalion colours showing on the arm near the shoulder. To our surprise the girls stopped us and one of them said, 'Please excuse us, you're returned men from the Eleventh Battalion aren't you?' We replied that we were. Then one of the girls said, 'We are from Bunbury.' Addressing me she said, 'You resemble a boy we knew who enlisted from Bunbury.' I replied that I was with a lot of boys from Bunbury at Gallipoli and I mentioned several. Both girls knew the names that I mentioned. I then asked the girl who had spoken to me her name. Now. What a shock I got. She said, 'My name is Evelyn Gibson.' Straight away my mind went back to the trenches at Gallipoli, and a pair of socks that I had received along with a note wishing the soldier who received it the best of luck and a safe return home to his loved ones, signed 'Evelyn Gibson, Hon. Secretary, Girl Guides, Bunbury, W.A.'

Although I had never had any real schooling, I knew what the word providence meant and that here it was now. Evelyn was the most beautiful girl I had ever seen. I felt as if I had known her all my life. I was really overwhelmed but I managed to suggest that the four of us go and have a cup of tea and a sandwich and talk about the boys from Bunbury. The girls agreed. They wouldn't go to a show with us later because they had to be in at the lodge they were staying at by nine o'clock, so we took them home. After that Evelyn and I often met, and when I had to stay in hospital she used to visit me as often as she could.

Evelyn and her friend would travel up to Perth on the Friday night Bunbury 'Rattler' and then return again on the same train on Saturday night. They would come and visit us in hospital. And that was how Evelyn and I started our courtship. Later she got a job as a live-in house-keeper in Mounts Bay Road and we were able to see much more of one another.

I was confined to bed often during the next sixteen weeks or more. Then I went before a medical board and was told that I was unfit for further military service and that I would be discharged and put on a war pension. I was advised that I would have to be very careful as the board couldn't guarantee that I would live more than two years. They said that they could be wrong so I shouldn't smoke or drink intoxicating liquor. This gave me a shock as I had proposed marriage to Evelyn and she had accepted me. I had seen her parents and they had given their consent. I felt very sad as I couldn't expect a girl to marry me under such a cloud. I decided to let Evelyn make the decision. That night I told her and she said that she wanted to go on with the marriage; she didn't believe the board's decision. 'Anyway,' she said, 'they are not sure, so we will continue our engagement.'

In June 1916, I qualified as a Tramways conductor. My war injuries were worrying me quite a lot but I managed to keep going, and after a few weeks Evelyn and I decided to go ahead with our marriage plans. We fixed the day for August twenty-first at Saint David's Church, South Bunbury, at eleven o'clock in the morning.

The wedding went off without a hitch and we had the breakfast at Evelyn's parents' place. It was a small, quiet affair; the war was still on and two of my brothers had been killed — there were so many sad and worried people at that time. After the breakfast we left by train for the city and the small house we had rented in East Perth. Our honeymoon was quiet — I took only one week off work and we had the time together at home. Then it was back to work for me as a tram conductor.

Three weeks later we had a lucky break. An employer of the Tramways, who was going wheat and sheep farming, offered to sell us his small four-roomed house in Victoria Park at very easy terms.

The price was four hundred and fifty pounds — no deposit — to be paid off at a pound a week free of interest. The house was build of timber and iron and was on a two acre block. This was considered a bargain so we gladly accepted.

Our first baby was born during the Tramways Union strike — on the third of February 1919 — and it was a son. We called him Albert Barnett (Barney). My wife and I were very happy.

The new conditions made my job much better and more pleasant. I liked being a motorman and my nerves had improved a lot.

I also began to get involved a little in the Union organization at this time. Everyone who was in the Tramways had to be a member of the Union and once you had your ticket you could attend meetings and so forth. I had my ideas about the way things should be done and started getting involved in the meetings and giving my views.

When you get active among men, and start talking about one thing and another, they begin to encourage you to get more involved. I was eventually appointed by my fellows to the Union Committee and I enjoyed this work a lot. I was able to get on well with everybody and felt that I contributed something to the Union. It also gave me another interest and helped to make the job with the Tramways more interesting and worthwhile.

Western Australia had an outbreak of a very severe kind of flu in 1920. It was called bubonic influenza and it killed dozens of people. I got it, but only in a mild form and we were quarantined for three weeks. I was away from work for a month and it was many months before I felt well again.

On January twenty-eighth 1921, our second baby came along. It was a lovely little girl we named Olive. My wife and I were very happy. Evelyn loved babies and she was a very capable person. She made all their little woollies and clothes and dressed them beautifully. I used to feel very proud of them and we went out as often as my job would permit.

We had a terrible experience in June of that year. I was feeling very ill and the doctor announced that I had diphtheria. They sent me by ambulance to the Infectious Diseases Hospital and my wife and children were again quarantined, this time for fourteen days. I was in hospital for three weeks and after that I didn't seem to recover properly, so I arranged for an appointment with the Repatriation Department. The doctor gave me a thorough examination and told me that I would have to leave the Tramways. He warned me that if I didn't anything could happen to me. He advised me to get out of the city and into the country.

When I told my wife the bad news she sat silent for quite a while. We puzzled our brains as what to do for the best. She reminded me that it was nearly five years ago that the same doctor and six others had given me only two years to live. I carried on working with the Tramways until we decided what to do. Then all of a sudden it came to me one day while I was at work. The Government was settling returned soldiers on the land and as I had a lot of know-how about wheat and sheep farming, I thought I stood a good chance of being selected. When I went home and explained the idea to my wife she thought it was the answer to our problem. I had been losing weight and also a lot in wages because of sickness. On a farm I would be my own boss.

We were the first couple to be registered as man and wife under the Soldier's Settlement Scheme. The property was valued at this time at three thousand pounds and the limit on finance allowed by the Board for one soldier was two thousand pounds, so the Act was altered to allow the wife of a returned soldier to come in as a partner, and the allowed amount was then four thousand pounds.

So we sold our home in Victoria Park and I gave notice and finished working on the trams. We packed our furniture and effects, and a carrier carted them to the Perth railway yards and loaded them into a wagon.

We arrived on our farm late in July 1922, too late to put any kind of crop in. My wife, who didn't know anything about wheat and sheep farming, was amazed at the size of the place. After we settled into the house (it had only been built two years), which was four-roomed, weather-board lined with dressed jarrah board, and a roof of iron, we spent a whole week having a good look over our farm and planning what we would do.

Finally we decided to fence as much of the cleared land as was possible and purchase some sheep to graze on it as soon as we could. So we purchased wire and wire netting, and while waiting for this to arrive, we both worked hard putting up the fence posts to hold the wire. My wife worked as hard as I did. By the end of August we had two hundred acres fenced and ready.

The annual Wickepin Agricultural Show was always a highlight in our lives. The children who were old enough to exhibit used to enter all sorts of things — farm produce, sewing, cooking, flowers, and so on. If they won any prizes, which were always announced towards the end of the day, they would line up to collect the prize money and then rush off to spend it before it was time to go home.

Evelyn used to be sewing for weeks before the show so that the children would all have new outfits for the occasion. They always looked grand. (We had five children by 1927 — Joseph was born in that year and Barbara was born in 1925.)

Our evenings were also very pleasant. We'd all sit around and play cards and other games and listen to gramophone records. One day while I was in Wickepin I bought a battery operated wireless. The children were delighted by it. We particularly looked forward to sitting down of an evening and listening to a serial about farm life called *Dad and Dave*.

As the children got older I also used to enjoy gathering them in front of the fire in winter and reading stories to them. One of the favourites was *Lasseter's Last Ride* by Ion Idriess.

Our children were wonderful and were always a great joy to Evelyn and I. We were very proud of them.

Early in 1935 I applied for a position as a trolley-bus driver and was accepted. I had to attend a school twice weekly in my own time to learn about trolley-buses and their workings. Then I had to have a written test, and after passing that test I had several driving tests and I finally got my licence to drive trolley-buses. This was much easier than driving trams as it was done in a sitting position and this suited me better on account of my war disabilities. And I also got more money.

Just before taking on trolley-bus driving Evelyn and I purchased a four-roomed house and four acres of land in Tuart Hill, a suburb north of Perth, on very easy terms — one hundred pounds down, then one pound per week, free of interest, and the total purchase price was five hundred pounds. This place was six miles away from the depot so I was still able to ride my push-cycle to work.

We settled into our new home. It was only four-roomed, but by enclosing the front verandah we managed to find enough sleeping space for the eight of us. We were able to grow our own vegetables and the man that we bought the property from had quite a quantity of fowls which were sold to us with the property, so we had our own eggs. This helped us quite a lot as my wages averaged four pounds per week and our budget was very tight. My wife managed quite well and I often wondered how, but I always got plenty to eat and the children were all well looked after and content. Evelyn was wonderful — she knew all the things required for making good palatable meals, and what she knew about making children's clothes was something you would have to see to believe.

Barney was still working for the market gardener in Wanneroo. He had settled in well and was not living at home now. He had grown into a very fine specimen, very tall, over six feet.

All our children were helpful and good. Our third son, Joseph, was an extraordinary boy. We used to give those that were old enough to go to the pictures on Saturday nights, a shilling each. That was sixpence to pay their way in to the pictures and threepence to buy an icecream at the interval. Many times Joseph would bring the threepence change home and give it back to his mother.

One thing that we all used to get a lot of fun out of was playing cricket. We used to play in the side-road next to the house — there wasn't a lot of traffic about in those days — and all the neighbouring children would join in. I would pick two sides and we would have a real game of cricket. We used to look forward to this as it was a family affair — with

Evelyn, our children, the neighbouring children and I all joining in the excitement.

We were always a little short of money. My pay was now averaging five pounds a week, sometimes a little more, and out of this five pounds came one pound for the payment on the house, Road Board rates and insurance, and then there were the usual school books, clothes, boots and many small expenses. My wife was truly a genius when it came to making money stretch to cover all our needs. We were a close knit family, each member helping the other. To help us with finance our second son George and our third son Joseph, who we all called Joe, used to go caddying at a golf-course about a mile away from our place and they always used to bring home a few shillings. This happened at weekends and on holidays when the golf matches were on. Evelyn taught the girls to sew their own dresses and so most of our clothes were home-made. This was quite a saving for us.

Early in 1939 we got the shock of our lives. Our youngest child, Shirley, was now seven years old, and one day Evelyn quietly informed me that she was going to have another baby, and sure enough, it arrived on September twenty-first — a son, Eric — and what a time Evelyn had bringing him into the world. We nearly lost her. I haven't ever seen so much suffering and pain, as the doctor wouldn't help her. He didn't believe in giving anything to ease the pain. He insisted that she should go through the thing in agony. What a doctor! After that confinement and after Evelyn had recovered from the ordeal I took no time in getting rid of that quack, that so-called doctor. Our son, luckily, was fine — he was a lovely child.

A few days before Eric was born World War Two broke out — our eldest son Barney was twenty now — and our worries commenced again. At first the Federal Government called for volunteers for the three armed services. Our son volunteered and joined the Second Fourth Battalion, Western Australia. He was training for several months, and then his unit finally sailed to Singapore and Malaya. They, with other units, were sent to try and stop the Japanese who were moving down through Asia to capture Singapore.

I tried to join up again but was rejected, so I attended an air-raid wardens' school and got an air warden's certificate. I was appointed as an air-raid warden in charge of the Tramways Depot. I was also a St John Ambulance man. I had many years of service as an ambulance attendant and for long periods used to voluntarily assist once a fortnight with casualties at the Perth Public Hospital. I received much knowledge in the handling and care for the injured. I also attended a Home Nursing class and obtained a Home Nurse's Certificate.

Our second son George also volunteered and went into training. After their initial training there was some considerable delay before his unit went overseas. George, a wild boy, ever in a hurry, couldn't stand it and so he stowed away with a couple of mates on a troopship taking another unit to Britain. When they were discovered they were brought back, punished, and eventually sailed with their own unit to New Guinea.

It was difficult to see our boys go off, knowing what they would be going through. I said to my wife when the war broke out, 'What do you think?' and she said, 'Well, I suppose they will want to go.' I went to the first war with my brothers without a second thought so I knew that they would want to do what they felt like. I said to Evelyn that whatever they wanted to do they should do. 'If they want to go they should go, if they don't, that's fine, but it is up to them.' We agreed on that.

When they did go I felt very sad, and so did Evelyn. But we knew that they had to do what they wanted. And it was terrible while they were away — we would always be looking for every bit of news we could get. We would ask people we knew that had boys away if they had heard anything. We would read all the papers. Anything that might give us an idea of what might be happening. Every morning the paper would have lists of dead, missing and wounded, and that was always the first part of the paper we would read. It was a terrible time for us.

It was during the years of the Second World War that my wife went through a change of life. It was a very bad time for her. When Singapore fell Barney was reported missing and we didn't hear anything of him until just before the war ended — nearly four years. It was a terrible strain, with Barney missing and George in New Guinea. Then just before the war ended Joseph had joined up. All this added up to my wife having what they called a slight stroke. One side of her face fell and the feelings on the other side of her body weren't functioning properly.

I don't know how we got through the four years that Barney was missing. We used to be hungry for news — if we overheard anyone saying anything which sounded interesting we'd listen in and ask them questions. We would have given anything just to find out something.

Evelyn was beside herself with worry. I felt bad but I had expected it. I knew casualties would happen because I had seen so many at Gallipoli. I knew that they would be lucky if they got through it. I used to tell her, 'Look, what's going to happen will happen — it happened to me — just when you least expect it.' I told her that we could receive news any day and I think that helped her. We knew then, from the start, that the chances were that something would happen and one of them might be killed.

Evelyn would sit down at the kitchen table to write to Barney while he was missing and tears would run down her face onto the paper while she was writing — not knowing if the letter would ever reach him. It was a very trying time for the whole family.

We were all involved in the war. We spent our time helping to raise money for the Comforts Fund to send things to the men in the battle areas.

Dances were held and popular girl competitions organized to raise money. Barbara joined the Land Army which was made up of girls who were willing to go and work on the farms in place of the men who had enlisted. She went to a dairy farm in Capel in the south-west of the state. She met her husband there and married in January 1945 and went to live in Bunbury. Olive had already married in January 1943 and had left home. During the last years of the war only Shirley and Eric were at home. It was a lonely, sad time.

Then on May twenty-third 1945, whilst I was at work, I received word that Barney had been killed on February fifteenth 1942 during the fall of Singapore to the Japanese. He was driving a truck when it was bombed in an air attack. It received a direct hit, killing Barney and four others. He was twenty-three.

Although I had expected this news I was devastated. I didn't know what to do. It was Evelyn's birthday that same day and I had organized a small surprise party for her and bought a present. I also arranged for a birthday call to be made on the radio — something to brighten her day and lift a bit of the sadness. I decided, after a lot of thought, that it would be best not to tell her and go through with the party. I thought it best for her to have a little bit of happiness because once she knew about Barney it would be a long time before she would be able to be happy again.

It was very hard carrying on and keeping it to myself and late that night after the party I told her.

It was the worst time of our life. She collapsed, it was too much for her. It was terrible, and I didn't give my beautiful wife and life's mate much hope of getting over this shock. But she did.

Our youngest child, Eric, was now nearly six years old. He was such a bright, lovely little boy and his lovely, cheerful little ways and winning smiles helped his mother to recover. Evelyn treated all the children alike — she thought the sun shone through them.

On August fifteenth 1945 the war ended. We were overjoyed and relieved. George and Joseph came through all right. Evelyn was on top of the world when the boys came home.

By 1946 all the Australians who had managed to live through the war and the prison camps were home. Although they had tasted victory and were very proud, their thoughts seemed sad. They were all down in the dumps, especially those who had had the misfortune of being a prisoner-of-war. They had had a very raw deal from their enemy, the Japanese. They were starved and badly treated.

People do terrible things in wars, in the name of their country and beliefs. It is something that I find very sad and frightening.

In November 1960 our youngest son, Eric, was married — so now all our children, except Barney of course, had gone on to other lives, and to families of their own.

Then in 1967 we were up-rooted by the Government's Main Roads Committee when they wanted to remove our house for a proposed new road. They paid us a good price and we moved to a house closer to the centre of Midland — closer to a doctor and chemist.

The following year my wife became very ill and she was sent to hospital several times, for weeks at a time. I engaged several different doctors but she never got much better. She seemed to get worse as the years went by and she had several blackouts. Then, on the eighth of July 1976, she became unconscious and stayed in that state until the third of August 1976. She died at seven o'clock at night in my arms. We had been married for fifty-nine years, eleven months and twelve days. So on this day the loveliest and most beautiful woman left me.

Evelyn had changed my life. I have had two lives, miles apart. Before we married I was on my own. It was a lonely, solitary life — Evelyn changed that. After our marriage my life became something which was much more than just me.

I now wish to end this story. On the thirty-first of August 1977, I will be eighty-three years old — another birthday. The loss of my lovely girl, my wife, has been a terrible shock to me.

I have lived a very good life, it has been very rich and full. I have been very fortunate and I am thrilled by it when I look back.

(Abridged from *A Fortunate Life*, an autobiography. This edition published by Penguin Books Australia, 1981.)

MARCELLA POLAIN
NEW

In those first weeks, so many things were strange to Hovsanna that, although people were polite and welcoming, she felt as if — when she had finally slept in the dark night before her wedding — she had not yet woken, and that everything that had occurred since bore the edge of dream. Each day convinced her even further, for each day she caught, at least once, in the timbre of a voice or a bell, in the angle or colour of light, in the shape of a stone or in a stranger's glance, something so heightened that the glance or stone or bell could not simply be itself.

It was as if she had done what she had always imagined, what she had heard, or overheard rather, in conversations between men and schoolboys, and entered a book, a world full of meanings she could feel and see but could not read. And each night, when she lay still beside him and allowed the day's final event — and its most strange — she wondered if tomorrow, when she woke, she would at last be back in her father's house, in her wide white room, with her little sisters asleep on either side and the smell of coffee and the baby's squeals winding up the stairs to her.

It was on one such occasion, while her husband was again lifting her nightdress, that Hovsanna began to wonder if other people would ever stop looking at her. They were respectful enough, never gazing for too long and often averting their eyes as soon as she noticed them. But it was the frequency that was beginning to trouble her. Was there something wrong with her? Did they know something she did not? What was it they were trying to tell her? Were they watching to see if she would realise she was still sleeping? Or, she suddenly thought, was it that she carried with her all day long that which was happening now? That, despite her careful washing and dressing, she carried a scent or a sign upon her that betrayed her?

She knew by now what her duty was, and by now, too, she was accustomed to it, even if she had been silly at first. It had been — well, a surprise. But he was right — she had learned quickly. It seemed to her there was nothing much to it. It was clear enough: they each had their role and, quite plainly, she had the simpler. Surely any fool could manage it. It was, at those times when they retired, only her husband's enthusiasm she struggled to understand, his urgency and humourless concentration. And, she gathered, something like pleasure — although she wasn't sure about that, for sometimes in those last few energetic moments when he cried out, it was almost a cry of someone lost or afraid. And he was often so exhausted then that he lay weak and trembling and struggling for breath, like someone in shock, and she felt concerned for him, listening, as she must, to his heart banging within the broad chest pressed against her ear. Eventually, he would raise himself from her, as he did now and, resting on his side or on one elbow, kiss and stroke her hair. Later, when he sleeps, she will get up and wash herself and rebraid her hair before creeping back to bed. But now she looked up at him looking down at her, and smiled at him, not knowing what to say. *You are a beautiful woman*, he murmured, and kissed her lightly on the forehead before he turned away to sleep.

Once, with her head tucked under his arm as it must be on these occasions, he being so much taller than she, and her face turned away slightly, she could see both the rising moon and the rise and fall of his flank, palely illuminated. And it was at this time that she began to laugh. Or perhaps it is truer to say that this was when she felt the first stirrings of something she was afraid could be laughter. Somehow she knew this, that whatever it was for him was no laughing matter, and she certainly didn't want to laugh. But laughter is a most contrary beast, not easily discouraged and given to revealing itself at the worst possible moments. So, the more sternly she tried to banish it, the more determinedly it grew in her so that, when she reached out, as she sometimes did, to hold onto the bedclothes while he finished what he was doing, throwing his head back and crying out again as if to God, she felt her body begin to shake. And there was nothing she could do about it.

It took him a few moments but, all at once, he was off her and looking worriedly into her face and saying, between pants, *What is it?* and *What's the matter?* And Hovsanna, her hand pressed to her mouth, was nodding. *Are you sick?* he said. *What's wrong? Shall I bring my mother?* And she, shaking her head, turns away from him, pulls the bedclothes over her head, opens her mouth and laughs out loud, louder than she can ever remember laughing. She laughs and laughs until she hurts, and then clutches her belly, gasping, *Ow, ow,* between the subsiding spasms of her laughter.

Benyamin is all the while just as he was when he last spoke — on his knees beside her, his white nightshirt twisted about his hips. When Hovsanna, her back still to him, is finally quiet and his involuntary smile has slipped away, he waits as if transfixed for her to turn back to him, to explain. But she is looking at the moon. If it has changed at all in those minutes, she thinks, it is perhaps just a little brighter, a little higher.

So it was, for some days, that Benyamin lay as still beside his wife as she lay with him until, at last, his mother, sitting beside Hovsanna on the roof garden in the evening, told her that in the absence of Hovsanna's own mother, Hovsanna should consider her husband's mother as her own.

If there is anything difficult in your married life, any questions you may have, perhaps I could help you. We are both women, after all.

Hovsanna nodded.

And my son seems ... not himself these last days. A husband, especially a new one, needs his wife, you understand.

Hovsanna glanced up momentarily from her needlework. Her husband's mother's needles clicked steadily, the concentration on her face undisturbed.

I, too, she said, *was once a new wife.*

Hovsanna nodded again, her eyes intent on the thin brass needle, the evening cool on her cheeks.

But my husband, God give him rest, and I were both new. For you — well, it must be different for you. I have told my son he must be patient. He must remember his first marriage. Men have memories like cheesecloth and hearts like glass. Be kind to him. He will come back to you.

Hovsanna's needle carefully separated the weave in the hem of her husband's trousers, drawing together the required threads into one stitch and the next. She quietly cleared her throat.

Mrs Vartevarian, she said. *Why do they cry out?*

The older woman paused a moment, laid her needles side by side in her lap and picked up the skein from between her knees, unravelling another yard of wool with a long, slow arc of her arm. Then, clamping the skein in her skirts, she picked up her needles again, eventually saying, *Everyone receives something from this. It is pleasure to them and, through their pleasure, God gives children to us. And we all want children.*

Hovsanna guided her needle into the next stitch and then the next.

Yes, she said, at last. And then, *Must they cry out to have children?*

No. Sometimes they cry out, sometimes they don't. But they must have the pleasure. Women, too, can sometimes cry out.

Oh. Must women cry out before children can be made?

No. It is not essential. Some women cry out, others never do.

What makes women cry out?

Mrs Vartevarian stilled her hands and looked at the girl. Hovsanna's glance flickered up to the older woman's face and away again. Even in the now failing light, Mrs Vartevarian could see the sudden sweat and colour on her face as she gazed intently at her work.

Is there nothing ... you enjoy ... in it?

Staring resolutely into the torn threads, Hovsanna searched for the right answer.

If there is, you tell him, Mrs Vartevarian continued. *Otherwise it might take him a long time to realise it for himself. My son is a clever boy but he is also a man, and men, well ... When I was new, I was frightened, and I cried, and my poor husband, who was also new, was at a loss.* She laughed. *Nothing he said or did could convince me. He spoke to his father. I spoke to my mother. It took weeks. My father became so angry. He was afraid they'd send me back. He spoke to the priest, oh dear ... it seemed like everybody knew.*

But they didn't ... send you back.

Oh, no. My husband was very good. For a while we ... had an arrangement. He showed me how to ... help him.

Help him?

Yes. There are different ways a man can have pleasure.

Oh? What ways?

Ways. And then one day there was a pitcher of wine in our room. The priest gave it to him, I think, although I never asked. And, well, then it wasn't so bad.

I've never had wine. Did it make you cry out?

Oh, no, laughed Mrs Vartevarian. *It was giving birth that did that.*

And Hovsanna laughed, too — although, if someone had asked her why, she could not have answered them.

(From *The Edge of the World*, a novel, 2007.)

NATASHA LESTER
JUST LIKE THE HEART

Dan

Alix — my mother — met Dan — my father — at an exhibition of his sculptures. And, as coincidence would have it, Alix met her lover, Jack Darcy, at an exhibition of my father's work too, albeit some time later.

A friend of Alix's invited her to the opening of an exhibition by an up-and-coming sculptor. Alix had gone along to the show because she liked free champagne and smoked salmon bites, not because she had any interest in art.

She noticed the sculptor being double-cheek-kissed and back-patted by women wearing pastel Chanel, women whose hands were stacked with rings like an abacus. He smiled at the Chanel women — too nicely, Alix thought, because surely an artist should be more cynical about such whimsical patronage. She was sure the Chanel suits and overringed fingers wouldn't be around if he was just another poor artist starving in whatever sufficed for a garret during those postmodern days of the early eighties.

Then, rather than study him, she'd studied his work. He'd used plaster — a material she'd only ever thought of as a healer of broken bones — to make sculptures of bodies, or not even bodies, but parts of bodies. Body parts not quite broken yet not quite whole. A set of toes without a foot, for instance. A knee, sitting alone, so that it didn't appear to be a knee, as if it needed the context of shin and thigh to make it be a knee. And a mouth, all thin stretched lips and openness as if it were struck to death whilst shouting.

Alix had been staring at that mouth, really staring, she knew, so that she hadn't even noticed him step up beside her.

'What do you think she's saying?' he asked.

'Something no one wants to hear,' Alix replied, then shrugged at the sound of her thoughts accidentally voiced. 'You're the artist; what did you want her to say?'

'Maybe she's saying yes to the man who's asking her out to dinner tomorrow night.' He smiled at her. 'Are you free?'

'Well,' Alix hesitated, 'as she seems to have lost her voice, I'll have to step in and say ... yes.'

The night of her date with Dan, Alix stood in front of the mirror wearing a shirt and knickers, wondering what she should wear to dinner with an artist who, according to her friend, had made at least one hundred thousand dollars on opening night by selling plaster body pieces to the women in Chanel suits.

Everything in her wardrobe seemed too plain or conservative or clinical even, so Alix took out the blow-dryer and concentrated on her hair instead of her clothes, examining the colour as each section began to dry. She wouldn't allow herself to be considered a redhead — although others often described her as such — because her hair was really a motley orange colour, like ripe mangoes. It was this orangeness that she would like to get away from.

She was sure that her life would have been different if she'd had distinctly red hair. Redheads were showgirls, dancers or queens. Unfettered jobs with irregular hours, irregular pay and a certain attitude. A redhead would have been to Africa instead of just talking about it. A redhead would have bought the Bvlgari necklace she saw every day in the window of the shop down the road because a redhead would not have to worry about whether it would offend the eyes of the relatives of the almost-dead everyday at work.

Alix finished blow-drying her hair so that it sat in a sleek, smooth line at the bottom edge of her shoulder blades. She turned away from the mirror. Besides, none of her patients would trust her if she had properly red hair. They'd think of other women, shape-shifters, whose red hair foreshadowed their deviousness — Orlando, Ophelia, Elizabeth — because red was a fluid colour even at the same time as it was strong. It was the colour of scalded skin; it was the colour of love in a clichéd heart.

'Congratulations,' Alix said as she slipped into the seat beside him at the bar.

Dan put a glass of champagne in front of her. 'Hope you like champagne. It's all I've drunk for the last twenty-four hours. It's not too often your show gets described in the *Herald* as the best of the year.'

Alix took a sip from her glass. 'So you're drunk and arrogant. Fun date.'

He looked at her for a moment then said, 'I'm neither. Just truthful. But yes, it should be a fun date.'

Alix ran her finger through the ring of water droplets left by her glass on the surface of the bar. She glanced at him. He was tall and blond and blessed. So she chinked her glass against his and said, 'To a fun date.'

He smiled, finished his drink and moved his body closer to hers. And there it was. A shiver of skin, like breeze drifting through the night of her dreams.

'So what do you do when you're not going to art shows or out with arrogant artists?' Dan said.

'I'm a surgeon.' Alix knew that information often ended such conversations. It wasn't feminine enough. Men seemed to prefer nursing, or teaching perhaps.

But he asked the next logical question. 'What kind?'

'I'm with the new heart transplant unit at St Vincent's.'

'I'd love to watch you do one.' He grinned. 'Now I sound weird.'

'It's not the kind of thing men ordinarily want to watch me do.'

He laughed. 'I mean for my sculpture. I like body parts.'

She finished her drink. 'Whole bodies too, I hope.'

Alix went to Dan's studio after dinner. Although, she thought, 'studio' was a word too poetic to describe the triangular attic at the top of his flat. It had very little furniture, just an armchair and a desk. Most of the space was taken up with white figures, like the ones she had seen at the exhibition the previous night.

'Plaster breathes,' Dan said, taking her hand and placing it along the torso of a figure of a woman.

Alix felt moistness beneath her fingers, a dampness rising like sweat from the white rock.

'It takes the moisture from the air,' he continued. 'That's why I like to work with it. It's not lifeless.'

Dan's hand traced her fingers, which rested still on the plaster woman. 'But if the moisture in the air disappears, she begins to desiccate. To thirst. And then she becomes too fragile to shape.' He touched Alix's arm, then her collar bone, the middle of her chest, and stopped to rest at her belly button.

To turn around? To move? To stay where she

was? Before she could decide, he lifted the hem of her skirt and moved his hand up along her thigh; he found the top of her knickers and slid his hand inside, over the thin line of hair on her pubic bone. Then he traced a path downwards, pressing lightly, circling around and around, increasing the pressure by the slightest increments until Alix felt her legs part because he wasn't pressing firmly enough nor circling quickly enough and so she began to move backwards and forwards against his hand, to rub, hard, and she came just as his other hand found her nipple and his mouth tasted the skin along the back of her neck.

Six months later there was a wedding, a house in Elizabeth Bay for the now famous and wealthy sculptor and his heart-surgeon wife, and a year or so of bliss.

Alix
Bliss. For Alix, it was the kind of bliss she had always imagined Cinderella and her prince must have shared in their happy ever after, the sort of bliss that came after the full stop, that was never written about because it was too private and also indescribable — how could something as simple as words on paper be capable of depicting this?

Take their honeymoon. Europe of course. Gorging on art. And then the discovery of a small gallery down a lane into which they had only ventured because they were lost, but didn't care because what greater delight was there than to be lost beneath the sun in Florence with the person you loved, holding hands, kissing, desiring, finding your way out only because then you could do more than kiss, more than run hands beneath the backs of shirts, more than feel one another through a filter of clothing.

Dan had seen the sign over Alix's shoulder. 'Another gallery?' he asked and she shrugged, not caring enough to say either yes or no.

But, walking inside the gallery is a scene Alix will remember later, when Dan lies dying, and she will understand that they were not lost, that something, fate if you will, had made them turn down that lane and into that gallery, the walls of which were hung with masks. Death masks.

Alix didn't understand what she was seeing at first until Dan told her. 'Some are made from plaster,' he said, indicating the far wall, 'and these ones are made from wax.'

Alix moved in close, so close that she could see or imagine, she wasn't sure which, the faintest etchings of the fine hair that covers a person's cheeks. 'It looks like the wax is lit up from behind,' she said.

'Wax soaks up light,' Dan said. 'See how the skin looks almost moist.'

'Yes.' Alix paused. 'Some of these faces look more alive than the people I treat in the hospital every day.' She looked up at Dan. 'When I see things like this I wonder what being dead really means. The moment I take out someone's heart on the operating table, they're dead, really — a machine is keeping them alive until I can stitch in a new heart. But I look at this mask and it's a person. I can almost feel them breathing. If his wife walked into this gallery and saw his face here on the wall she'd think he was still living, surely?'

'They used to take death masks of unidentified bodies. That way, if someone came looking for a missing person, they could view the death mask and see if it was the person they were searching for.'

'What about just to keep someone with you, forever? A mask is more reliable than memory, more immediate than a photograph.'

Dan stepped closer, ran the backs of his fingers across her cheekbone. 'Are you saying you'd need a mask to remember me after I died?'

'You're not allowed to die. Ever. Besides, I'm a heart surgeon. I can fix anything that goes wrong.'

The house in Elizabeth Bay straddled their two worlds of real bodies and plaster bodies. The hospital was just a short drive away and Dan had a studio built, separate from the house, at the back of the garden.

He worked when she worked and so their life worked, perfectly. If she was called in at midnight then he would get up too, go to the studio and sculpt until she returned home. Then they would cook breakfast together — always bacon and eggs, mushrooms and toast because working at midnight made them both ravenous. Then they would collapse into bed in a flurry of arms and legs and hips and backs before finally falling asleep, waking whenever it suited them to go out for dinner or to a gallery. He sustained her, made it possible for her to work twenty hours straight at the hospital because he did the same, they did everything the same; sometimes Alix forgot that there had ever been a time before Dan.

Then there would be a few days when she would work normal hours. Go to work at seven in the morning, come home at seven in the evening and not be on call at night. She loved those days, loved stepping into their house and feeling the warmth — Dan always kept the heater on high and so Alix only ever wore T-shirts, even in winter — but she cherished the fact that he did because when she opened the door and felt the rush of hot air, that was when she knew she was home. The house smelt warm too; the ginger tea that he drank with the commitment of a caffeine addict fragranced the air, as did the pot of soup he'd reheated for lunch, or the vegetables he'd roasted for dinner. And the wall in the hall that he'd insisted on painting amber did have the effect he'd said it would — she'd thought of Betadine when she first saw the colour — but when it was finished and every time she came home she thought of welcomes and friends and drinks and Louisa. Then there was him. Dan. She could feel the heat of his art, his inspiration, scalding the air, could almost see it firing on his skin. She could hear it too, in the rasp crackling over plaster, the fall of dust onto the floor.

She tried hard to understand his world — the slurry of white paste and the way he transformed it into art, working away on it long after she thought it was finished, until he'd made it into something more than she could have ever imagined it would be — because he was the only person who understood Alix's world. She would often take him into the hospital late at night and show him things, because who else could she talk to — the only woman in a team of alpha males.

She took him up to the roof where she had stood for the first time as a surgical resident, watching the row of green traffic lights and the two police cars, sirens slicing into the quiet of night, speed to the hospital with a heart on ice in an esky in the boot. She told him how she felt as she raced down the stairs to tell the surgical team that the heart had arrived, intoxicated with the thought of the power she might have one day as the surgeon stitching in the heart, rather than being, as she was then, so inferior as to be often overlooked, happy to have been given a job — even one as lowly as being the runner on the stairs — and not fighting for once to be that most impossible thing — a female hoping to be a heart surgeon.

Occasionally, Alix would take Dan into the anatomy lab at the hospital late in the evening when she knew the interns would be gone. She introduced him to her cadaver, the one she practised on every day, knowing she had to be more than perfect if she wanted to be a heart transplant surgeon — she had to be peerless.

The cadaver was a man, aged about forty she guessed, slightly overweight, covered in hair and sporting a curly black mullet on his head. A man whose heart she knew better than anyone's.

Dan jumped when she snapped on the lights in the lab and she laughed. 'They're all well and truly dead, especially now that they've had interns hacking into them every day. They're not about to leap up and tickle your neck.'

As she finished speaking her hand crept up and brushed his neck. He jumped again, then grabbed her hand, laughed, pulled her towards him and stopped. 'I don't think I can kiss you in front of dead people,' he whispered.

'You don't have to whisper, they definitely can't hear you.'

He smiled. 'Maybe if I pretend that this is a studio and the bodies are sculptures or something.'

Alix unzipped a white body bag on a trolley and nodded. 'They are sculptures. As a surgeon I get to find the beauty in them that no one else sees. Like the thinness of the wall of his atrium. If it tears, you die. But mostly it doesn't. I have an old T-shirt that's about the same thickness and it's full of holes.'

Dan stepped up beside her and Alix could see that he had become used to the smell of formalin, that his eyes were no longer focussed on the tattoo of a butterfly that sat in the middle of the man's chest, asserting the fact that he was once a person, an individual who chose, for a particular reason, to have a butterfly drawn between his lungs.

'Show me,' Dan said and his face had become the one he wore when he was working, the expression in his eyes that of a concentrated dream.

Alix took his hand, just as he had done in his studio the night of their first date. She pulled back the incised skin, lifted out the pre-cut ribcage and plunged his gloved fingers into the opened thorax. She moved his hand as she spoke. 'Here are the four chambers of the heart: right atria, left atria, right ventricle, left ventricle.'

She stopped moving his hand, looked up at him and continued. 'I like the word chamber. It makes me think of bedchamber, a private space, a lovely space. Just like the heart. The filling and pouring and looping of blood, the relaxation and contraction that must all occur, that usually does occur, in sequence, in perfect time over forty million beats a year.'

Dan ran his hand over the surface of the heart. 'What does it feel like to touch a heart that's still working?'

Dan was the only person she knew who would ask, who would think of such a thing. She leaned over and kissed him, reflecting on how unromantic the situation should be — two people with their hands stuck in a dead man's chest — and almost laughed. Then she answered him. 'In surgery you get to feel what it is that makes a person alive.'

For the first time in her life, it occurred to Alix that the feeling was similar to love.

(From *If I Should Lose You*, a novel, 2012.)

TRACY FARR
TRICK THE LIGHT

We met at Circular Quay. Beatrix was dressed in trousers, wide at the ankle. I saw her first from a distance; she faced away from me, yet I knew it was her. She turned, as if she felt my eyes on her, and as she turned, the legs of her trousers swished and moved like the sails of a ship, revealing ankle straps on her glossy shoes. Her face was lit with a smile. She wore a white fedora over bobbed hair, powdered face and the reddest of red lipstick on her wide lips. Yet while her clothes and appearance were a mixture of mannish and womanly, no one could see her at that moment and not know she was a woman.

Beatrix doffed her hat, winked at me, walked towards me, rested her hands on both my shoulders and kissed me on one cheek and then the next, in the European way I was used to from the Professor and Madame Petrova.

'Ready darl?' she asked me, turning so that we faced in the same direction, towards the ferries, and taking my arm with hers. 'I took the liberty,' she squeezed my arm gently, 'of purchasing tickets for the two of us to travel. We're just in time. Hustle your bustle, doll.'

Whisked along as I would come to expect by Beatrix, we joined the flow of people boarding the ferry berthed at Manly Wharf. The day was fine, and we secured a position on the deck, sitting close together on wooden slats that bounded the cabin. Beatrix took a packet of cigarettes from her pocket, and offered them to me. I took one, and Beatrix leaned in and lit it for me, her hand around mine around the match to shield the flame from the breeze.

We talked about everything and nothing on the trip to Manly; and we watched the bridge.

'Look at it,' Beatrix said, 'God, it's so beautiful. I love painting it. Not just the bridge. The water, the light. The shapes. The spaces between the shapes. The way they change as we move past them. I like to try to paint that.'

From the water, the view of the bridge was different than from anywhere on land — from that low angle, looking up, it seemed so much larger. Its overall shape had not changed since my view of it from the *Houtman* as I'd steamed into Sydney for the first time. The shape was the same, but denser, spaces filled, lines and curves connected. It looked stronger, more permanent, even though still the two arcs of the bridge did not meet. The air around and between the arcs hummed and rang with the sounds of construction from the bridge, of human voices drowned by metallic ringing.

The air had been still that morning, heavy with humidity and unseasonal warmth for autumn. On the water, air moved past us as the boat moved through it, creating a cooling breeze. It felt like an escape, to be surrounded by water, by its sound. The sweat on my back, under my arms, dried quickly in the breeze. I felt light again, released from the dragging effect of the city. I wore the dress I had worn for my first meeting with the Professor: black and white, elegant. I felt myself cool underneath the dress, felt the fabric move against me.

The ferry docked at Manly and the crowd of disembarking passengers streamed off onto land. Beatrix — she had said again, on the ferry, *call me Trix* — Trix took my arm. Her arm was cool; I could feel my sweat slicken the soft underside of my elbow against her dry skin.

Trix walked us to tearooms that overlooked the water. We took a table in the rotunda, outside but shaded from the sun. She ordered tea, sandwiches, and cakes. We talked as we ate. I learned that she was an artist, a painter, and that — born ten years from the close of the old century — she was more than twice my age. Having long ago escaped from the cold southern town of her birth across the water in New Zealand, more recently she'd returned to Australia from living in Europe, in places with romantic names, Paris, Vienna, Berlin. I spoke of my music, of my conversion from cello to theremin, of my interest and delight in the modern. We were loud, sometimes, over tea that day. We were looked at, by quieter patrons. I rested my hand on the table; Trix covered it with hers, cool and slight.

We walked down past the hotel and on to the beach, shoes off, sand crunching and squeaking between our toes. I could feel the stretch in my calves, felt myself push against the hard wet sand low on the beach. Trix linked her arm through mine. The waves were quiet that day, not booming, just a light, rounded swell. At the western end of the bay, where the beach curved around, long shadows from Norfolk pines fell on the beach, formed strips of shade on the white sand. We fell in and out of darkness as we walked.

We caught a late, crowded ferry back to Circular Quay. People smelled of beer and oil and sweat and fish. Trix and I resumed our places at the front of the boat, where the air moved the smells away, and the boat thrummed underneath us with its rhythmic tug. We were quieter now, all talked out. We listened instead to the talk around us, talk of football and fish and Missus this and Mister that. We smiled at each other, smiled at the same overheard fragments.

I looked at Trix. The light from the low sun glowed. She reached for my hand, resting in my lap. As she reached, tucking her little hand around my long fingers, her knuckles brushed against me, pressed the fabric of my dress to touch me lightly, underneath. I glowed with the sun, with the touch, with heat, a spark in me fired.

We arranged to meet again the next day. I waited for Trix at Circular Quay, watched her step from the ferry and stride towards me. She placed her hands on my shoulders, brushed her left cheek first against my right cheek, then her right cheek — slowly — against my left cheek. She breathed out hot breath against me, spiced with cigarette smoke.

'I've brought lunch,' she lifted a large, worn velvet bag. 'And a little drink.' She linked her arm through mine, and we walked together. I matched my long stride to her smaller step. We walked for hours in the autumn sun, through The Domain, the Botanic Gardens. At Mrs Macquarie's Chair we sat and ate cheese sandwiches unwrapped from waxed paper, washed down with sherry from a tin bottle, all drawn from deep in her velvet bag. We sat close on the seat in the shade, so close I could smell the sherry on her breath. She lit a cigarette for me, and one for herself; she shifted closer to me, turned her body, just a little, so that she looked at me. We sat and smoked and watched the world, watched each other.

We walked back to Circular Quay late in the afternoon. Trix held her bag in front of her, low, almost dragging on the ground as she walked. As we approached the terminal, she turned to me, placed her hand on my arm.

'Come to my house. Come for tea. My paintings — I want to show you. Come on.'

We chattered up the hill from the ferry dock at Mosman to Trix's house in Royalist Road, leaning in on one another, giggling and scurrying like two schoolgirls. We climbed up the steps onto the verandah that wrapped around two sides of the house.

'Turn around, look!' Trix told me. 'This is where I paint, sometimes.'

From the verandah you could see the bridge. The shapes and curves of it, the two halves like the swell of full breasts, or pregnant bellies, reached towards each other, approaching completeness. You could imagine the arc the finished bridge would form; your eye drew it in, filled the space, completed it, connected the two pieces. We stood for a moment; I could think of no words to say. I could feel her next to me, and nothing else mattered.

The house was quiet, dark inside; no one answered Trix's *coo-ee!* as we slammed in through the front door from the verandah.

'Sherry? Mmmn, sherry, yes. Come on.' She took my hand and pulled me with her through to a lean-to kitchen where, on a shelf, bottles of liquid shone, next to glasses of every shape, none of them matching. They stood upon embroidered linen, next to candles in silver sticks, as if on an altar. Trix poured amber sherry into two glasses, one of panelled red glass, the other fine crystal. She handed me the red glass, clinked the crystal against it, and took my hand again.

'Come on. I want to show you.'

She led me down the hallway, through an open door. It smelled of paint, of turpentine, of smoke, of our sherry.

'Look,' she said, 'let me show you. The light. What we've been looking at. What I see. What I can make it do.'

She drew the curtain aside, let in the pale light of the dying day. The room was full of paintings. Canvas rested against canvas, some framed, most of them not. Paintings faced out into the room, or turned their backs to us, faced the wall. They were on the floor, on a bookcase, a desk. They hung on the wall, they sat on a well-stuffed chair by the window. She lifted one — small, barely bigger than the width of a dinner plate — and held it to me. I took it from her.

It was the bridge viewed from the verandah. Somehow, though, I could see it not just from the verandah, but from the ferry, from the other side of the harbour, from Mrs Macquarie's Chair, all at once; all of those views and angles were combined. The painting was all about movement, and shape. It swam before my eyes.

'But how?' I said. 'How do you — how does it move like this?'

She took the painting from me, kissed my cheek — just shy of my mouth — and placed the painting on the chair by the window.

'Ah, see, that's why I wanted to show you. It's what I do. I trick the light.' She held her hands wide, inviting me, enticing me to move around the room. I looked at canvas after canvas of the bridge, the rooftops, the sky and the water. Still lives — the altar of wine and glasses — cigarettes and matchboxes. People I did not recognise, their faces and bodies formed in shapes and planes and colours.

'And this, look at this. Ah, it's old, but still —'

A cello was fractured into parts; not the parts of a cello, and yet somehow, combined, they made me know they formed a cello. The dun colour of the wood was enlivened, shot through with blue, light reflecting from glass under the instrument. It stood by a window; that was it, a window. Or was it water? I couldn't tell.

'I used to play — before the aetherphone — I played cello.'

'You told me.'

'It's beautiful. But I don't understand how you do it.'

'I interpret what I see. This is how I see the world. This is how I make it look.'

The cello in the painting was a cello, and yet not a cello.

'It makes me think — of the sound I make with the aetherphone. Not like a cello, but like it. Both more than it, and less than it, at the same time, and yet itself as well. I'm not making sense, I —'

'No, no, it makes sense. I think that's it exactly. Itself, and more than itself, and less. Everything connects.' She stubbed her cigarette out in a bowl on a table. 'Everything connects!'

She moved towards me, took the empty red glass

from my hand, placed it on the table next to the ash-filled bowl. She reached up to place her arms around me, her hands hooked over my shoulders and her fingers reached under my chin, their touch gentle.

'Beautiful girl.'

I breathed in, almost could not breathe out. My face turned to the left and I kissed her finger.

'Oh.' She made a noise like *tsk*, with her mouth. 'Beautiful, beautiful girl.' And she raised up on her toes, and I leant — just slightly — downwards, and we kissed, our lips light at first, then heavy upon one another, smoky, sweet, intense.

We fell into one another. Beatrix took my body and fractured it into parts, so that I felt every part, every piece of my body with an intensity that was new to me, delicious. I felt the parts put together into a whole that was greater than it had been, before Trix. All of the planes and curves of my body were showing, all at once, inside me and outside me and all around me.

(From *The Life and Loves of Lena Gaunt*, a novel, 2013.)

CRAIG SILVEY

CHELLOW

The evening is cool and suffused with an apricot afterglow. A fresh breeze breaks. To the east, the moon is out with a herd of early stars. As though they have crept stealthily from the ether to watch the sunset.

Eleanor moves along the pavement among a tedious traffic of diligent pet owners. She knows the way. She can smell barbecues and sprinklerspray. Cars interrupt games of cricket played on warm asphalt. Kids are sent outside to eat watermelon. She walks past a waft of pot and patchouli, a woman calls out and asks if she'd like her tarot read. She declines politely.

Her chest is taut and her breath short. Her period bites sharp. She bumps her dog with a friendly thigh.

What the hell am I going to say, Warren?

He guides her from the low barkless arm of a devious sheoak, which waits patiently to clothesline the blind. The light has aged to a spread of vermilion.

The gate is open. She weaves up the path. Smells bougainvillea and mint.

She is peered at by a bashful gnome, a leaning saffron sunflower, and two inquisitive possums on a verandah beam, still alive. She walks underneath them. Stands on a prickly unwelcome mat.

Eleanor knocks through a slab of air. A door-shaped hole. Warren sniffs. She raps the thick architrave, an inaudible thud that stings her knuckles, taxes some skin.

Silence. Her bare shoulders goosebump with breeze and nerves.

Hello? Hello?

The possums turn around, their eyes wide and glassy, their tails intertwined.

Ello?

She hears a scuffle and a sniff. Doesn't see the tall figure that emerges slowly. Ewan squints, groggy and stiff. Puzzled by his slumber, the open door, the red twilight sky, her. Dazed he traces the path of her long shadow that reaches down his hallway to touch his toes.

Hello?

Warren doesn't like the smell of this place. He backs up, warily watching the man down the hall. He tries to look thuggish.

You're there, I know. I can hear you. Door was already open.

Still. Silence.

Eleanor feels her pulse thumping. Almost hears it bashing against her sternum. A rash of heat across her face.

Look: I was just, well, I just wanted to sort of atone, okay? I'm sure it must be unnerving being stalked by the blind, but I'm quite safe, really. And I'm sorry that, you know ...

She tails off. A pause, thick with discomfort.

This is going well isn't it?

Ewan is very still and very quiet. He does not blink. She tries again:

My name's Eleanor anyway. This is my warren, Dog. She flushes. This is my *dog, Warren.* And it's just, that, whatever it is you play, like, your instrument, it's just ...

Silence.

Still.

There is weight on her instep. Whatever it was she wanted, she didn't come here to make an arse of herself. She lingers for one more breath. Swivels. Warren responds with enthusiasm. The sky is stark crimson. She turns back. Sharp. Fuck it.

She steps inside, feels smooth cool floorboards. The smell of stale air and mothballs. Heaves it in.

For my birthday this year I baked myself a sponge cake and I whacked a candle in it and got food poisoning because the eggs were off and I had a flu so my nose was blocked and so I didn't know. I gave it to Warren. Whatever. You want statistics? I'm a twenty-one-year-old virgin and I go for days without sleep because I have bad dreams that wake me up just in time to piss myself. My surname is *Rigby* for fuckssake and I have a mother who is addicted to television and I'm tired of minding my *own* business. No. I'm just *tired*. And do you have any idea why I would want to like, come to your house and tell you this? No, of course you don't, and neither do I. Neither do I. Jesus, I mean, I just don't *do* this. And I don't know *why* whatever it is you play here helps me to sleep, I don't know, *soundly*, but it does and I don't know why. I really don't. But, you know, I know it must be hard, but you really don't have to avoid me okay? I'm blind so I don't really respond to body language too well. If you want me to piss off just say so. Trust me, I'm resilient, I'll be okay.

She feels strangely lucid. Out of breath. Delirious.

Silence.

What are you, bloody *mute*?

The sky is a sheet of fading mauve. She opens her mouth again. She's interrupted.

Cello.

She swallows. His voice is baritone, soft and all of a sudden. Young.

It's what I play. The cello.

Cello. Chellow. Well, it's nice. It's really nice.

Silence again. She feels her slim momentum slipping.

So, wots your name?

Pause.

Ewan, he says, even softer.

Ewan. Well, it's nice to meet you, Ewan. She smiles. Ewan. Yoowen. Sounds like something you'd do to a sheep, doesn't it. Doin the Ewan.

Pause.

Sorry. She rubs a palm into her forehead. My *God*, I sound like Bruno. Sorry. She laughs nervously.

In the dark, neither of them can see. Eleanor takes up Warren's harness and she's suddenly bold. Her voice is resonant down the hall.

You know what, Ewan? Nobody has ever taken me out to dinner. I think you should. Yeah. I think you should. She smiles, chirpy. What do you think? Tomorrow then? Good. Good. So I'll be round, what, seven thirty?

Silence.

Still.

Good answer. Okay, well, I'll see you then. Bye.

And she's strolling back down the path; quick, before it catches up with her. She just leaves it there, hanging. And Ewan does not interject, hasn't the time.

Two possums watch her leave with four wide eyes. They are smiling.

Ewan slowly flicks a light to make sure she has gone.

Thick steam rises in the shower. It has the sweet taste of tin as she breathes it in.

Eleanor twists taps, Hot and Cold, slides a curtain, sniffs. And that shaft of humidity follows her out like a creeping fog.

The bathroom is an ugly spread of lemon and lime and white tiling. The cream grout is stained umber in parts. There are two mirrors. One in front of her, one behind. But being blind means she can't see her body on reflection. Front or back. So she doesn't see the fresh sheen of her skin, or the colour of the crusty towel she is reaching for (grey). She doesn't see the whiteness of her small pert breasts against her nutbrown arms. Doesn't see the two jutting bonebumps on her shoulders. Or the tuft of arrowed hair that she's touched but never seen. Or behind her, the corrugated arc of her spine, the deep dimples between her bum and her back.

Dry, she tortillas herself in the towel and opens the bathroom door. Leaves wet prints down the carpeted hall. Foot shadows; a record of pigeontoed steps.

In her room, she dresses quickly in clothes she has already laid out. Fast and systematic. In front of another pointless mirror. It's where she has always got changed.

Nervous and restless. She works her skirt a little lower on girlish hips. Makes sure her top is on the right way round and her tits are organised. Worms into her Peasant Birkenstocks. Moves back into the damp bathroom. Smells grapefruit bodywash and Estelle's talcum powder and pods of lavender soap. She feels about for her toothbrush.

It's Tomorrow Night. Around six. And Eleanor Rigby is squeezing toothpaste embarrassingly early. Ready, with an hour and a half to kill. And still rushing. Maybe even smiling as she brushes. Going too fast to get to thinking about the night ahead. Her empty belly roils and folds and cramps with tedious eggdispensing.

She spits foamy minty froth. It splats and gurgles. Rubs her face with a balding handtowel. Glosses her lips with lipgloss. Pats her pockets. Smoothes her bumcheeks with her palms.

Keeps moving.

Ewan is still in a coldblue Volvo when she knocks. His head turns sharp. His gut sinks.

He waits. Eyes closed.

She knocks again.

Ewan staggers sapless from the garage into his adjoining kitchen. His hair is dust tipped from the interior lining.

He can't do this. He stands at the foot of the hall. She knocks again. His hairs stand on end. The fan carves languid, like the shit's already hit it. Vertigo, that's what he feels. Heavy dread and the gnaw of nausea. The passage ahead is dim and turbid and hot. The air hard to breathe. He is basted in sweat. Lilian, the cello, is clear and garrulous to his left. Only he can hear. He glances and his feet lust to push her way. To pick Lilian up, to have her there like armour, like a shield. A sturdy abdomen.

She bangs the door. It rings down the hall.

Slowly, he wades forward. One step. Two, three, four steps. Shuffles. He takes harried, fragmented glances at his Options. From that room, to that door. And back again. And back again. And back again. Why can't she just leave? Just fuck off and leave him be, leave him alone.

She thumps the door. Hello? You there, Chellowboy?

He is. Standing. Barnacled to the floorboards. His head, back and forth and back and forth. Forth. Forth. Like he has a choice. Where to run now? Out of his skin? In a circle? Up and down this dimly lit vestibule? No. He can't, he's mired in this, ineluctably, he knows.

All of a sudden he wants to sleep. To lie down and cup his skull and sleep.

She belts the door. He sees it bow concave. He can reach it, pull it, but he can't.

Hel-low!

Ewan folds and hobbles back a step. Head pounding.

Hey! I know you're there. Hurry up. This is just rude!

Bile is wedged solid in his gullet. And it's forward he moves as two horny possums scratch and wrestle and squeal to climax above him. His thumb snaps a latch. Fingers meagrely meet a doorknob, greasy with sweat, shaking. A shudder gusts from his spine.

He opens the door to a Blind Girl and the breeze she brings. To light and unsteadiness.

The first thing Ewan notices are her eyes. Bright blue and dead set. They crinkle a little at the edges to make room for the width of her smile, the second thing he notices. Her lips are lacquered and thick, parting for a burst of sudden white teeth. She has a tiny nosestud. Her hair is short and indecisive, sometimes tamped and sometimes scruffy, sometimes tawny sometimes blonde. Her long ears give an elfin look to her face.

She wears a thickstitched navy denim skirt that somehow hangs from her thin hipbones, breaking into a fray just past her knees. Thin shoulderstraps cling to her cowlneck top, its deep henna red augmenting her tan. Tight enough to suggest her bra-less breasts, loose enough to conceal her ladder of ribs. A tag flaps at the nape of her neck.

A slab of her stomach is deep brown, with a thin white strip below. She has nutty, nubby toes with crustyskinned edges. Her feet are slightly inverted.

How long did you take in there? God, you're like a woman. Hope you didn't make yourself too beautiful. I must confess, I was a bit early. I have been sitting on your verandah for the last half-hour. So: you ready then?

Silence.

He can't do this. He wants to scream at her: No! I'm not ready! I'm not fucking ready! The farthest he has strayed from here in six years is Bruno's Cornerstore, and that was only yesterday. On his boldest days, he opens his bedroom window three inches. The rest are rusted shut. And shuttered. No. He can't.

But being blind means she can't see the stricken expression that is just *there,* or the blatant weight of his feet pushing back, back, back. Can't see the fear in his wide eyes, in his poise.

No, he says quietly, I'm not ready.

You're not? How come? Her smile eases.

Silence.

Two postcoital possums take their afterglow for a stroll onto the verandah beam. The breeze swoops in.

Shoes, Ewan says. I need shoes.

Well put some on! God! Are you *sure* you're not a woman?

Ewan scuffles stiffly back down the hallway. Looks for shoes. Or red ruby slippers. Eleanor follows, inviting herself in with the dog at her heels.

Shit, how tall *are* you anyway? Sounds like, what, six-seven? Six-eight?

Silence.

Well, let's just say tall then. You're a tall man, Ewan.

Ewan finds his shoes. He kneels dizzily.

He feels surreal and emptied. Stoned, almost. Strangely separate from his senses, as though his vision, his hearing, his flesh is orbiting distantly around him. Far far away. Hazy and incongruent.

Shoelaces. He concentrates on shoelaces. Eleanor breathes in deep.

Your house smells like mothballs. And pot, she says. You should air it out.

He doesn't appear to hear. The dog is sniffing the length of his shin, eyeing him carefully. The hallway is lucent and clearing with the breeze she brought. Fine dust shifts. There is someone else in his house! A girl, and a dog, and the door is gaping wideopen! His jaw clenches. He can't do this.

Pull. Loop. Tie. Pull. He sneezes. The dog flinches and backs up.

Bless you, she says.

Thankyou.

You're welcome.

He stands, feels like retching. Looks at her. Why are you here? he asks. Soft. Almost a whisper.

Her head tilts up. Because you're taking me to dinner. You ready now? It's all right, I'm paying. You just have to *take* me. Can you do that?

Silence. He pleads with a look of unease.

Good. She nods and slips back down the hall, her steps perfectly linear. Her small calico bag swings. Ewan is hesitating. Warren is sniffing a skirting board. He licks it. Eleanor waits as patiently as she can at the threshold. Still inabighurry so she doesn't give ground to doubt.

Ewan grapples with faintness. Implosion. His head is aching and his chest compressed. He exhales. Absently he grabs a nugget of rosin. Pockets it.

Walks. He's level with her now. The horizon is garish with melty hues. The possums are peering from above. Eleanor drops the harness, ushers Warren inside.

It's all right if I leave him here, yeah?

Sorry?

Warren. He'll be all right here won't he? She feels a pause of complaint. He should be fine, really. He's very well behaved, aren't you, Warren?

Warren sits and looks confused.

Ewan is very still, and very quiet.

Let's be off then, she says. They stand on a prickly unwelcome mat. You going to close your door?

Ewan slowly closes the door. There is piercing noise in his head. Now, don't be alarmed, he hears her say, but I'm gunnahafta grab your arm, okay?

She clasps his arm just above the elbow. He feels the heat through his shirt. Touching.

Thankyou, she says.

They turn. Careful down the steep steps. And their legs are brushed by squat unkempt shrubs as they edge through the centre path together.

(Abridged from *Rhubarb*, a novel, 2004.)

ANNABEL SMITH
DELTA

Charlie found out about *Delta of Venus* on the first day of term because his twin brother Whisky had been friends with Grainger, who owned the book. But he didn't actually read any of it until a couple of weeks later, by which time every boy in the school was talking about it. Grainger had been on holiday to France and claimed to have bought the book from a kiosk, an ordinary kiosk, selling newspapers and chewing gum and cigarettes. It was a well-known fact that France was a land of sex maniacs, that you could buy things there that you couldn't possibly get your hands on in England and there were plenty of other boys who'd come back from holidays with dirty French comics. But Grainger's book was different. For starters, there were no pictures. In theory when you read something dirty you could make up your own pictures. But some of the scenes described in Grainger's book were beyond Charlie's imagination; he could find no place for them within his own concept of sex.

Not that he would have called himself an expert. At the age of fifteen, sex was one of those subjects that you pretended to know everything about whilst knowing almost nothing. If you asked questions you were exposed, tainted with the word *virgin* and would never live it down. Finding out more without risking exposure, that was the challenge.

Charlie had no sexual experience of his own to speak of, except for a fumbled kiss with Michelle Perry in a cupboard at a party, during a game of Spin the Bottle. Other boys had come out of the same cupboard with different girls and much better stories to tell. Tom Costello had put his hand up Louise Barker's skirt, Chris Lennox had felt Claire Corbell's breasts and, allegedly, Charlotte Graham had put her hand down Joel Orton's pants.

Would things have been different if it was Charlie who had ended up in the cupboard with Charlotte Graham? Would she have put her hand down Charlie's trousers — down anyone's trousers? Or did Joel possess some skill which Charlie had not yet mastered? Could Charlie have touched Michelle's breasts if he had tried? How did you know if a girl would or wouldn't? How could you change her mind?

These were the questions which plagued Charlie, questions which he could not ask and could not find the answers to: not in the encyclopedias and medical books at the library; not in their father's awkward and incomprehensible talk about *the birds and the bees*, not in the explanation they had been given in health education by the dried-up, flat-chested Miss Pennacombe, who, it was agreed, could not possibly ever have had sex herself and therefore could have nothing to teach them. Certainly her interminable description of the sperm fertilising the egg had done nothing to help Charlie decipher the dirty jokes he heard, though he always laughed anyway, hoping he was laughing at the right moment.

He thought he understood the mechanics of it, the what-goes-where. But that, to Charlie, was not sex. Sex was what he had seen in the dirty magazines boys at school had pilfered from older brothers or stolen from newsagencies. Or at least, that was what Charlie had thought, until he read what was inside Grainger's book.

Delta of Venus, that was the title. Nobody knew what it meant exactly, no one could have used the words in a sentence, but they were passed from boy to boy, muttered and snickered over until they came to represent everything you needed to know about sex and didn't know how to find out. Very few people had actually seen the book. Apparently it had a very sexy cover: a picture of a naked woman, but not like a centrefold, more *arty*, so that you couldn't see her face; in fact, you couldn't even be sure which part of her body you were looking at though you had a pretty fair idea. After the first week, no one got to see the book at all, apart from Grainger's close friends, Whisky included, who confirmed for Charlie that the rumours about the cover were true.

All the other boys ever saw were the photocopies. Grainger made the photocopies at his dad's office on a Saturday morning and at school on Monday you could buy them for 20p a page. You couldn't choose which parts you wanted, it was the luck of the draw. But according to Grainger, who claimed to have read the whole book, there wasn't a page that wasn't dirty so it really didn't matter which one you got.

The first week he made twenty copies and he'd sold them all before lunchtime on Monday. The following Saturday he made a hundred copies and he put the price up to 50p. It didn't matter if you'd paid 20p the week before; 50p was the new price, take it or leave it. You weren't allowed to show them to anyone else or swap them and anyone who tried to make their own copies wouldn't be sold anymore. Those were the rules. No one argued. Everybody wanted the photocopies and Grainger was the only one who had them. They were shocking and disgusting and he got rid of a hundred in two days. With the help of Whisky and his friend Joel, he sold them before school and after school, between classes, at recess and at lunch, in the toilets and behind the bike shed and on the school bus. Even when he made a hundred and fifty copies there still weren't enough to go round.

Charlie did not have to pay for the photocopies because Whisky got them for free, as many as he wanted. Charlie had mixed feelings about this set-up. On the one hand, he was relieved that he did not have to buy the copies himself. Once he had read a few, he knew that there was something wrong about them, something that made him feel guilty and shameful. Charlie suspected he was not the only one who felt this way. He noticed that though everyone was talking about the photocopies, no one actually talked about what was in them. You bought them, put them in your bag and took them home and when you came to school the next day you said, I got the baron and the little girls, or, I got the woman and the dog. But you didn't talk about the things you read.

The story of the man who pulled the corpse of a naked woman out of a river and then had sex with her dead body was disgusting to Charlie but when he read it his penis got so hard it was almost painful. There were sentences he read over and over again until they got stuck in his mind and he couldn't close them out. Charlie had rubbed himself raw over the story of the Cuban and the nymphomaniac and for days afterwards one sentence went round and round inside his head. On the bus and in his maths class and at the dinner table it would come to him unbidden — *She was moist and trembling, opening her legs and trying to climb over him* — and it took all of Charlie's willpower and concentration to control his erections.

There was nothing you could say about that. So you didn't talk about the stories with your friends, you didn't talk to anyone about them. Even when he got the copies from Whisky, Charlie couldn't meet his eye. The thought of buying them at school, like the other boys had to, was unbearable. He was sure that if he had to make that transaction, in front of other people, every one of them would know what he was thinking, what he did alone in bed at night once the light was off. So he was grateful to Whisky for sparing him that humiliation.

At the same time he resented him for once again being at the centre of something that Charlie was on the outside of. For although it was Grainger's book, Grainger was part of Whisky's gang which meant that in the eyes of everyone at school, Whisky was as much a part of it as Grainger himself: Whisky had seen the book, knew the story about where it had come from, was helping Grainger to sell the copies — it might as well have been his own book. Whereas Charlie, as always, was on the sidelines; hadn't so much as glimpsed the book, didn't even have the gumption to buy his own copies but had to get them second-hand from his brother and for that, Charlie hated him. For he knew that this book was just the beginning, that in sex, as in sport, Whisky would be Charlie's superior, that he would go further faster and Charlie would be left behind, as he had always been since the day they were born.

Delta of Venus dominated Charlie's life, all their lives, for a little more than four weeks. In the fifth week, Whisky, Grainger and Joel were caught selling the copies in the science block toilets and the jig was up. The book was confiscated, presumed destroyed; the boys were caned and suspended and the proceeds of their sales, which totalled almost two hundred pounds, were donated to the Salvation Army. The situation was evidently too scandalous to be handled by a woman — the special assembly, for the boys only, was addressed not by their headmistress, Mrs Aster, but by the deputy headmaster, who also happened to be the head of religious education. There was barely a boy in the school who wasn't implicated and the hall had never been so still or silent, two hundred and fifty pairs of eyes trained resolutely on the ancient woodblock floor as Mr Daniels spoke of his *shock and disgust* over the confiscated materials and his *disappointment at the lack of moral fibre* evidenced by this incident.

The assembly lasted less than ten minutes, long enough for Whisky, Grainger and Joel to be made an example of, long enough for the same fate to be threatened to any boy caught in possession of such filth.

The shit's going to hit the fan, Whisky joked to Charlie on the way home, but Charlie knew that Whisky feared their mother's reaction more than any punishment that could be meted out at school. To be caned was not a humiliation but a badge of honour, a sign that you'd been outrageously rebellious, and as such earned you the respect of the other boys. As for the suspension, Whisky looked upon it more as a reward than a punishment.

Though the boys knew their mother must have had a telephone call from the school, she was ominously silent when they arrived home. They slunk off to their rooms, assuming she was waiting for their dad to come in from work before she made her move. But at dinnertime she still said nothing, only glared at Whisky, and at Charlie as well, as though he too was implicated, though she could not have had evidence of that. Or could she? Charlie prayed that she hadn't found his photocopies, wedged beneath his mattress.

It wasn't until Whisky attempted to excuse himself that she finally spoke.

Sit down, William, she said in a low voice. What have you got to say for yourself?

Whisky shrugged, keeping his eyes on the table.

Look at me when I'm speaking to you.

Whisky looked up but said nothing, knowing from experience that whatever he said would only make matters worse.

She looked at their father. Bill, do you have something to say to your son?

This surprised Charlie. Their mother was the disciplinarian, that was the accepted order of things. These were obviously deemed to be special circumstances as they had been at school; a man-to-man matter. But Charlie could see that his father was unprepared, stuck for words.

Not one of your better ideas, Whisky boy, he said eventually.

Their mother stared at him expectantly, waiting for him to go on. He let out a sigh, appeared to be thinking hard and then he began nodding his head; something had come to him.

Certainly very entrepreneurial though, I'll give you that.

Charlie cringed.

His mother exploded.

That's right Bill, encourage him, that's the idea! Your fifteen-year-old son is producing and distributing pornography and you tell him he's entrepreneurial! For pity's sake, is there anything at all between your ears?

All right, Elaine, calm down. I was just trying to have a joke. Whisky knows he's done the wrong thing, I don't think we need to labour the point.

Labour the point? She laughed then, a sharp abrupt sound like the bark of a dog who has been unexpectedly shut outside. No, you're right, of course, we shouldn't *labour* the point, better to make a joke of it, give him a pat on the back and with any luck he'll leave school at sixteen to become a pimp, is that what you want?

Charlie was shocked to hear his mother use the word *pimp*. He sneaked a look at Whisky but Whisky wouldn't meet his eye.

Don't be ridiculous, Elaine, you're overreacting.

Overreacting? Do you have any idea how many times I've had William's headmistress on the phone this term? He can't stay out of trouble for five minutes. I'm at the end of my tether!

Bill coughed. Well, perhaps you're right. But the boy's already been punished; I don't think there's any need for us to get heavy-handed as well.

Their mother snorted. One week off school! You

call that a punishment? She turned her attention to Whisky. Charlie did not often feel sorry for his brother but he felt sorry for him then.

There'll be no bike-riding, no skateboarding, no television, no Atari. No phone calls, no hanging around at the shopping centre, no listening to your records. And you won't be seeing your partners in crime, that's a certainty.

Whisky was flattened. What am I supposed to do then?

There are plenty of ways you can make yourself useful around the house, I can give you a list so long you won't have time to scratch yourself. And woe betide you if you defy me, William, because I'll find out, believe me, and then you'll really know the meaning of the word punishment.

By the time Whisky got back to school, the whole thing had blown over. Once the book was gone, the source cut off, the fever subsided. When people stopped talking about them, the photocopies lost their currency; Charlie gave up reading them, left them for weeks under his mattress, eventually threw them away.

Sex became once again about the girls you knew and how far you could go with them. As in the American movies they watched, progress was measured in *bases*. Since they had never played baseball and no one knew the rules, there was some confusion about exactly what happened at each base. First Base was kissing, that much was generally agreed. But to Charlie, even First Base was a grey area. Because as everybody knew, there were two kinds of kissing.

There was the kind of kissing that took place during a game of Spin the Bottle, in which you were shut in a darkened cupboard with a girl you may or may not fancy (and who may or may not fancy you, although this was considered largely irrelevant) and you had thirty seconds to locate her mouth and work your tongue inside it. To Charlie's mind, this kind of kissing had more in common with Pin the Tail on the Donkey than with baseball and he did not know if it counted as First Base.

He suspected that First Base meant the kind of kissing that happened at upper fourth parties, where no one played Spin the Bottle anymore, but people somehow paired off anyway; the kind of kissing where you locked lips with a girl and didn't come up for air until you had attempted to touch every square inch of her body with your roaming hands. The second kind of kissing Charlie had seen plenty of but had never participated in himself, which meant that depending on one's definition, he had never even got to First Base.

Second Base had to do with breasts, tits, jugs, knockers, baps or whatever else you might call them. A lot of the girls in Charlie's year didn't seem to have much to offer in that department, at least not compared to the women in the magazines Charlie had seen. But if he had to touch a girl's breasts in order to progress to the next stage he was prepared to do so, even if the girl in question was as flat as a pancake.

By the end of the upper fourth, Second Base seemed to have been so widely achieved that it wasn't worth discussing anymore. A lot of boys claimed to have got to Third Base, some even further, while Charlie was still stuck on First. According to reports there were plenty of girls who'd let you touch their breasts or even slide your hand up their skirt. But Charlie always seemed to end up with the frigid girls, girls like Alice Brown, who had kept her lips clamped shut when he kissed her so that he couldn't get his tongue in her mouth, or Susan Wilkes, who had gripped his wrists while they kissed so he couldn't touch her body at all.

Whisky, of course, had already made it to Third Base. He had got off with Louise Barker at a party and then gone out with her for about three weeks, before dropping her because she wouldn't 'go all the way'. What he failed to take into account was that when you dropped a girl because she wouldn't go far enough, she would want to get back at you. And the best way to do that was to get off with someone you knew and go much further with that person, maybe even all the way, and then to make sure you found out about it. If she really wanted to get back at you, she'd get off with one of your best friends or, better still, your twin brother. Which is how Charlie, in a surprise twist of fate, managed to cover three bases in one night.

It happened like this. There was a party at Tom Costello's house in the first week of the summer holidays. Because Tom's brother was sixteen, there was beer at the party which meant that by nine o'clock, everyone was getting off with someone. Charlie was in the kitchen, swigging his beer as though he loved the taste of it, when Louise's friend Claire came over.

Charlie! Where've you been? I've been looking for you! She said this playfully, as if they were good friends having a joke together, which confused Charlie, because although he knew Claire by name, he had never actually spoken to her before.

Louise wants you, she said, conspiratorially.

Louise Barker?

Claire rolled her eyes. Of course, Louise Barker, who else would it be? You know she's mad on you.

Charlie couldn't make sense of this conversation. He thought he must be drunk.

But Louise went out with Whisky.

Whisky! Claire scoffed. Louise *hates* Whisky. You're the one she likes. That's why she asked me to come and find you. She wants to talk to you.

Where is she?

She's upstairs, Claire said, in the first bedroom on the left. She's waiting for you. And then she took the beer can out of Charlie's hand and gave him a little push towards the stairs.

Charlie went upstairs slowly, trying to work things out in his head. It couldn't be true that Louise liked him when only a week ago she'd been so keen on Whisky. Probably she wanted to talk to him about Whisky, see if there was any chance of them getting back together, ask Charlie to put in a word for her. But if that was all, why did she have to send Claire to find him? Why couldn't she come and talk to him herself? Perhaps Claire was setting Charlie up, perhaps Louise was upstairs with some other boy, or wasn't upstairs at all and the whole thing was a wild-goose chase designed to expose Charlie's desperation. But what if Claire was telling the truth and this was Charlie's big chance to make some progress on the bases? Charlie knew it was a long shot but it was this last thought which propelled him up the stairs and into the first bedroom on the left.

The room must have belonged to Tom's little sister; everything in sight was pink, except for Louise who was sitting on the bed on top of a Flower Fairies duvet cover.

Hello Charlie, she said, I've been waiting for you.

So that much at least was true. Charlie smiled, or perhaps grimaced, unsure of how to proceed.

You'd better shut the door, she said, and patted the bed enticingly.

Charlie sat down.

You look exactly like him, Louise said, staring at Charlie in a way that made him feel even more uncomfortable.

We're identical, Charlie said awkwardly. He hated it when people commented on how alike he and Whisky were. He especially didn't want to talk about it with Louise. But Louise continued to study him.

I think Whisky's a little taller, she said thoughtfully.

It was true, but Charlie was hardly about to

admit it. He wanted to get off the topic of Whisky altogether.

Claire said you wanted to talk about something.

Well, we can talk anytime. Wouldn't you rather kiss me? Louise said. And then she leaned forward unexpectedly and pressed her mouth against his. Charlie had a moment's hesitation.

It didn't seem right to start kissing without a little more chitchat. And given that Louise had just broken up with Whisky, Charlie probably shouldn't be kissing her at all. But she smelt like fruit salad and her mouth was so warm and soft that Charlie couldn't help himself. He leaned in closer to her but she pulled away to look at him again.

It's so weird kissing you, she said. I feel like I'm still kissing Whisky.

There they were, back to Whisky already. But then Louise pulled his face into hers as though nothing else mattered and side by side in that pink and sparkly room they kissed until Charlie couldn't tell where his mouth ended and Louise's began. Without knowing how they got there, Charlie found that they were lying down on the bed, and getting to Second Base happened so quickly he barely had time to take it in. Even the fact that he couldn't undo Louise's bra didn't slow them; she sat up and took it off herself and though she had hardly any breasts to speak of, her perfect pink nipples were as soft as her mouth and Charlie found that their size didn't matter at all. They were pressed thigh to thigh, hip to hip and Charlie had the biggest erection of his life.

When Louise looked at her watch and said, Imagine if Whisky knew what we were doing, Charlie knew something was wrong but when she undid his belt and put her hand inside his boxer shorts he didn't care, he didn't care. The feeling of Louise's hand wrapped around his penis was so intense, so consuming that he didn't even care when the door opened and he saw Whisky standing there, with Claire behind him.

Don't stop, it doesn't matter, Charlie groaned, feeling himself only seconds from ejaculating. But as soon as the door was closed Louise pulled her hand away and, seeing the look on her face, Charlie understood what he had taken part in.

It had all been for Whisky; Louise wasn't interested in Charlie at all. Now that Whisky had caught her with Charlie, caught her going further than she had with him, Charlie might as well not have existed. She didn't even look at him while she put on her bra and straightened her clothes. Charlie didn't care that he'd been set up, that Louise had used him. Those twenty minutes he had spent with her had been the best twenty minutes of his entire life. What he couldn't stand was that this moment, this triumph, was not his own. That even when he had overtaken Whisky it was Whisky who had helped him to do it, so the triumph, as always, was Whisky's.

(From *Whisky Charlie Foxtrot*, a novel, 2012.)

ADAM MORRIS
RENTAL

Saul had made a decision to rent an apartment. It was only a few minutes bus ride from his work. He had decided against buying the house and land package. He would still need to keep his job in order to pay the rent but he wasn't locked in for twenty years. It was a relatively good area. The apartment was a three-tiered building with about fifteen places on each floor. Some had two bedrooms, Saul's had one. He was on the middle floor, the people below him had a courtyard and stayed up late watching music videos; the lady upstairs wore high heel shoes on her hard wood floor and seemed to keep strange sporadic hours. Saul's plan was to stay in the apartment for a few months, keep his job for the time being, look for another one in the meantime and maybe buy an apartment in the block as there were always one or two for sale at any given time.

Saul had halfway gotten a few things together. He was even thinking of buying a car for himself. But as yet he still hadn't sold any songs, he hadn't played a gig for three weeks, and worst of all he hadn't had a girlfriend for what seemed like three years.

Of all the things Saul felt in his life — inadequate, broke, emotionally detached — it was his loneliness he felt most of all. He couldn't really imagine it ever changing either. Who would possibly want to spend their time with him? Who would want to spend an evening with him, let alone a lifetime? He was cynical, miserable; he wasn't successful in any part of his life. He was living and working towards a childish boyhood dream of being a successful musician and songwriter. What an immature ridiculous pathetic way to go through life. Each day that passed was another day he didn't make it. It was still the same: one leg in two different worlds and not a secure footing in either.

It was no wonder he hated everyone around him, he hated himself, he hated his lack of success, he hated his stubborn determination to keep persevering when there really looked like no end in sight whatsoever. No light at all, just an ongoing, lengthy, painful and lonely darkness. Maybe had he fallen to the floor in the minister's office, maybe that was the moment. Maybe his prayers were answered that day but he ignored it. He had felt like throwing himself to the floor. Saul thought they called it prostrating yourself. Maybe God had heard his prayers, heard his pleas, recognised his self-loathing and had taken mercy on him. Maybe God existed and maybe he took pity on Saul and said, 'All right I'm going to help this poor fucker out. I'll show up and let him know what's really important, I'll fill the room he's sitting in. I'll put him out of his misery.' But then Saul didn't prostrate himself, even though he felt he should. Not because someone told him, no one even suggested it, he just knew it, or he thought he knew it. What a state he had lived himself into where the possibility existed that he would ignore even God rather than look stupid in front of someone he didn't know. Saul now felt scared as well as lonely. Had he gotten blackout drunk one night and made a pact with the devil he couldn't remember?

He decided to go out.

Saul stood at the bar, it was quite busy. It was full of people who looked the same age as Saul but much happier. They were no doubt selling their songs thought Saul. That fucker over there looked very happy. That girl with her arms around that fucker's neck, staring into his face and smiling, she looked very happy too. Why did Saul do this to himself? Before he left his apartment he had played out a familiar fantasy in his head. He would stroll into the bar like it was his lounge room, he'd be as comfortable there as the guy who owned it. He'd sit at the bar, order a drink and strike up a casual yet clever conversation with the bartender, acknowledging his intelligence, skills and talents above that of an ordinary barman. The man would appreciate Saul's recognition; maybe even give him a few free drinks for his effort.

Then some woman would enter, she'd be looking for her friends, but they haven't turned up yet. She would have funky hair maybe braided tight across the top of her head, she'd be wearing a leather jacket, maybe a dark cherry-red, it would have a light brown fur lining around the collar. Her jeans would be tight, dark blue, spotlessly clean. She'd have high cheekbones, maybe blonde hair, maybe it would be raining outside and there'd be what looked like a light perspiration on her face. Her chest still rising and falling a little as she had to run to stay out of the rain. She'd be slightly flustered but not nervous or panicked. Saul would help her as she took off her jacket and fumbled slightly with her handbag. She'd be the slightest bit nervous about accepting his help but grateful. He'd pay her a compliment and she'd take it, take it well. He'd buy her a drink but the bartender wouldn't take any money. She'd be impressed and her friends wouldn't show up. They'd talk. For hours they'd talk. They'd drink and finally they'd kiss and her mouth would be warm and soft and she would smile while they were kissing and he would feel her warm breath in his mouth and his nose and they'd kiss more and fall in love and drink and kiss and laugh and drink and he'd be able to feel her clean dark blue denim jeans against his, and for that he would prostrate himself over and over again.

When Saul got to the bar all the stools had been removed. He had to squeeze through a mass of people all more successful, all better looking, all stronger, all happier, all having fantastic relationships and all selling songs around the world. It took another fifteen minutes just to get the bartender's attention. When he finally did, the barman couldn't hear him when he ordered a drink; he leaned forward with his ear looking pissed off. In the end Saul had to point to a beer mat on the counter and make a 'large glass' sign with his hands. The bartender didn't even nod, just went and got it. Saul had brought a lighter with him in case someone asked him for a light and maybe that someone was a beautiful single woman, but the pub had banned smoking since Saul had last been there. Maybe later he could set fire to the toilets.

Saul stayed at the same spot in the bar and watched people dance, jump around and laugh. It never rained outside, no beautiful woman came fumbling up to the bar, everyone's friends all turned up and Saul didn't fall in love with anybody. The lights flashed on in the pub and turned off again. That meant everyone had fifteen more minutes to finish their drinks, exchange phone numbers and make that move they'd been waiting to make. For Saul it meant his night was over and he should go home immediately and spare everyone else in the bar the painful spectacle of his presence. Saul drank the last of his drink and headed out the side door.

He had the same trouble hailing a taxi to get home as he'd had buying a drink in the bar. He started to walk. Cars full of people went flying past as he headed home. Cars full of laughter, Saul thought it may never come for him. He thought about his life, he had perhaps another forty years, maybe fifty. Then he'd be dead. And there'd be nothing left of him and there'd be nothing left behind him. This was no way to spend a life thought Saul. If there was no God, Saul was really making a lousy job of his life. If there was a God his life was an insult to the God that created him.

'What is Saul up to?' some angel would ask God.

'I've got no fucking idea what he's doing down there,' would be God's reply. 'He seems to be spending a lot of time filling out a daily time log,' God would continue with a bewildered look on his face. 'Really I haven't a clue what he's doing.'

'Do they know about death?' would be the angel's next question.

'I remind them as often as I can,' God would say. 'Sometimes I feel like that's all I do.'

Saul turned the last corner and headed in towards his apartment. He climbed the first set of stairs. As he reached his door he was searching for his keys in one of his pockets. When he finally put the key in the door the lady who lived upstairs made her way up the steps below him. She didn't look at Saul. She was a lot older than he'd imagined. She was fiftyish, slightly dumpy, and as she walked up the stairs he heard the familiar clop of her high heels. She looked slightly wobbly as she turned into the last stairwell.

Saul listened outside his door. Above he heard her wrestling with her keys, open her door and shut it with a bang. Saul did the same and headed in.

He turned on the TV and watched terrible video clips for terrible songs, one after the other. He poured himself a glass of wine. He had a slug of whisky while he let the wine breathe out. He stood in front of the TV. He didn't want to sit down, if he did he'd end up still awake on the couch at three in the morning with his hand down his pants and a bad smell in the apartment. He changed the channels, nothing. There was a horse-jumping show. A reality program about the lead singer from Poison. A Chinese period-movie which looked incredibly depressing: a small Chinese girl was sitting huddled with her little brother hiding from the rain under a porch; neither of them had shoes. They wore identical clothes. The little boy was crying, the girl was promising him things. Saul couldn't watch. He drank both his drinks. He quickly fried an egg and toasted a piece of bread over the gas flame on the cooker, he burnt it in some spots and didn't even toast it in others. He ate it. The egg was too soft, it ran down his fingers. He threw the frying pan in the sink, turned off the lights and fell into bed.

He lay staring at the ceiling. He could hear the lady above him still walking around her apartment. He imagined her cooking her own egg sandwich, going through her own late-night rituals. He wondered where she'd been tonight, how she spent her life. It was as if she was marching up there. Her heels pounding on the floor with every step, she kept retracing the same steps. What the fuck was she up to?

Saul heard her flop into her own bed. The apartments were all designed the same so she was just above Saul. He lay there as he listened to her flip and turn and then a sound cut through the ceiling with a low continuous hum.

Bbbbbbbzzzzzzzzzzzzzzzzzzzzzzzzzzzzzzzzzz zzzzzzzzzzzzzzzzzzzzz.

Saul was gripped by it. The woman upstairs was making love, sort of. And he could hear it. It didn't need its washing done, it didn't fight with her, it did exactly what it was told to do, it went exactly where it was told to go. Saul remembered Orson Welles in one of his old movies where his advice to a hapless soul was, 'Ask the machine.'

It went on and on, the way drunken sex often does. Except this time only one side needed satisfying, the other simply needed to be plugged in every now and then. The drone grew louder and a little higher pitched as the time went on. Saul listened as the lady pushed herself to the limits when all of a sudden the drone vanished, cut short. Silence. Saul hadn't heard any human noises to suggest a favourable ending. He waited. Then he heard. He heard the woman walk for the first time without her high heels, she bounded across the floor towards the room above Saul's bathroom. He heard a pair of knees hit the floor and then it all came out. A stream of vomit hit the water. One gush, then another, then another. A pause, Saul was awake listening intently. Saul thought it was all over until one more poured out of the poor woman into the bowl. Saul wished he knew how much money she had spent on what was now making her sick. How much time she had worked to earn that money, and how much she had enjoyed that time earning that money.

The toilet flushed, the footsteps made their way a little slower but a little more surely back to the bed. He thought of all the lonely souls sleeping tonight, falling asleep drunk, drugged or sober with another day behind them leaving them yet again unconnected by chance during the day. There was a great untapped potential for love out there thought Saul. Connections that were left up to fate, chance and opportunity. Where friendless souls could meet and fulfil the harrowing hole left by loneliness. Saul counted himself among them. He thought again of the minister's office, the touch that might have been, he thought of praying for the lady upstairs.

Then he heard it again. The hum of the machine droning back to life.

(From *My Dog Gave Me the Clap*, a novel, 2011.)

ELIZABETH JOLLEY
MR PARKER'S VALENTINE

After only a few weeks Pearson and Eleanor Page were tired of living in the rented house. The rooms were small and stuffy, and the repetitive floral carpet depressed them every time they stepped into the dark hall. Pearson felt his wife would be less homesick if they had a house and garden of their own.

'House hunting will do you the world of good,' he said to her. Friends of theirs, just as recently arrived from England, were happily settled already, busy with paving stones, garden catalogues and plans for attractive additions to their new home.

So Eleanor looked at houses and quite soon she found exactly what she had always wanted. In the evening they went together to see it. It was old and had an iron roof. Wide wooden verandahs went all round the house, and faced the sun, or were shaded at just the right times.

On either side of the street were old peppermint trees, and there was an atmosphere of quiet dignity in the decaying remains of a once well-to-do residential area.

There was, however, a difficulty about the house. They stood together with the land agent out in the back garden, surrounded by a wilderness of full-skirted red-splashed hibiscus and flower-laden oleanders. All round them tall trees in a ring, sighing now and protesting, tossed their branches in the afternoon sea breeze. Cape lilacs, jacarandas, flame trees and Norfolk pines, green, light green upon dark. And, nearly as big as the house itself, a gnarled and thickly-leaved mulberry tree, with early ripened fruit dropping, replenished the earth.

They stood in the noise of the wind, as if at the edge of waves, and were submerged in the swaying green, as if in water of unknown depths, to ponder over their problem.

At the end of the garden was a tall shed, stone-built with a patched corrugated iron roof. The door of the shed opened to the western sun and, in a little plot edged with stones and shells, herbs were growing and wild tobacco flowers. A short clothes line stretched between the door post and the fence. An old man lived in the shed.

'The trouble is,' the land agent said, 'he's lived here for years. The owners hope that whoever buys the house will let him stay on. He has no other home.'

'I'm afraid it's out of the question if we buy the house,' Pearson Page said, shouting a little to increase his authority and determination. He was a short man, fresh faced, looking younger than he was.

'Oh! I do so want the house,' Eleanor said. They stood remembering the recent pleasure of large fireplaces and polished jarrah floor boards, of high ceilings still with their graceful mouldings and, of course, the windows. Tall windows, each one framed and filled from outside with green leaves and woven patterns of stems and roses, jasmine and honeysuckle. And all the rooms so fragrant just now with the scent of Chinese privet.

'I never had a house with such a spacious kitchen,' Eleanor said, adding to their thoughts. She wanted the house very much and felt the old man being there could make so little difference.

They all moved down to peer into the shed.

A great deal was crammed inside the shed, an old man's lifetime of experience and possessions. Boxes were stacked and his lumpy bed was smoothed and tucked up in a black and grey plaid. Some matting covered the floor and there was a plain wood table and three scrubbed chairs. Over the wood stove were shelves piled with pans and crockery, and a toasting fork hung on a nail. Ivy, growing in under the roof at the far end, hung down in a dark curtain catching and concealing the full sun as it flooded in through the open double doors.

'Place would make a good biscuit factory,' Pearson tried a joke, as he saw disaster in the corrugated iron and an old man's clothes hung out to dry in the sun.

The character and possibilities of the house were overwhelming; Beethoven in the evenings and perhaps the writing of poetry. Eleanor longed for such evenings on the verandah. She stepped into the shed.

'Pity to turn the old man out,' she said. 'But it would make a marvellous rumpus room for the boys.' She used the word 'rumpus' with the self-conscious effort of fitting in to the phrases of a new country.

'Ah, you have sons?' the house agent asked gently.

'Yes, two,' Eleanor explained. 'They are just finishing off the year at boarding school in England and will be joining us later.'

'Mr Parker's out shopping just now,' the house agent continued in his soft voice, his knowledge suggesting years of experience of Mr Parker's habits. 'He does not trouble the house at all,' he said.

The wind tossed the tumult of branches to and fro. 'Think it over,' the house agent said.

The Pages had always enjoyed a single-minded, smooth partnership in their marriage and now, for the first time, they were unable to come to some kind of agreement about the old man and whether he should be allowed to stay.

'I can't think why all this fuss,' Pearson said, his face very red because of the sun; he scooped out the fragrant flesh of a rock melon. Juice stayed on his lips. 'We can buy the house if we want it. There's nothing about the old man to stop us buying the house. It can be ours tomorrow. All we have to do is to say we don't want him there. And he'll have to go. It's as simple as that. I can't think why you're so worried.'

'But Pearson, where would he go? We can't just turn him out. I couldn't live there if we did that.'

Neither of them slept.

In the end Pearson agreed to the old man remaining. 'Any trouble,' he shouted, 'and out he goes!' He did not want to disappoint Eleanor and, in any case, he wanted the house too.

On the day they moved in they were too pleased and excited at being able to unpack their own things at last to think of the old man.

Pearson strutted in and out of the empty rooms giving instructions. He was a sandy man and his face was fresh and rosy coloured, contrasting with the tired grey cheeks of the two men who were carrying in the furniture and the countless boxes; for Pearson and Eleanor had many books and pictures and other treasures.

In the evening the old man came up to the back door and introduced himself. He was small and clean and had the far-away voice of a deaf person.

'I've roasted a half leg of lamb, the shank end, I thought you'd like a bit of dinner. Six-thirty sharp, down at my place,' he said. 'Plenty of gravy.'

Eleanor in her dirty removal dress was embarrassed. 'Oh, no thank you. We couldn't possibly spared the time ...' she began, smiling kindly at his best clothes. But he could not hear her.

'Don't be late! Six-thirty sharp; hotting up a roast spoils it,' he said, and went off down the garden.

So there was nothing to do but leave their unpacking and arranging, tidy themselves up and go in an awkward little procession of two down to the shed.

Inside the shed it was surprisingly bright and cosy; it was the wood stove and the smell of the hot meat. The old man told them about his life when he travelled round Australia at the turn of the century. He was just explaining about the quarantine camps of those far-off days, when he suddenly stopped, and said, 'Yo' know what day it is?'

Eleanor, smiling, shook her head.

'Valentine's Day!' he said, and he climbed up on the boxes and fetched down a grimy envelope from behind a rafter.

'Fifty years ago that was sent to me,' he said proudly. And he showed them the dusty paper pillowed heart, stuck all over with faded daisies.

'Who sent it?' Eleanor asked. She had to shout the question three times, self-consciously, trying to hide Pearson's boredom.

'Ah! You're not supposed to know who sends a Valentine,' the old man creaked with the far-away reedy laughter of the deaf.

Late in the night, they made their way up the dark garden. The house, neglected, was hostile with nothing done. Confusion in every room.

'Not even the bed made,' Pearson's voice was disagreeable with the wasted evening. He had wanted to put up pictures and arrange their Venetian glass.

'Oh Mr Parker's delightful.' Eleanor hurriedly

found the sheets. Really Pearson's sulky ways made her very uncomfortable, especially as the old man was so friendly.

In the next few weeks there were some things to trouble them. Old Mr Parker, early one morning, painted all the verandah posts blue, spoiling the appearance of the house.

'Protection against the weather,' he explained. He chopped down the passion vine, his thin stumpy arms whirling the axe as if he had unlimited strength.

'Too old,' he pointed at the gnarled twisted growth of the vine.

Every time Pearson started to do some gardening, Mr Parker was at his elbow.

'Wrong time of the year to prune them lemon trees,' he said. And, 'Yo'll not pull up all them bricks in that path, I hope.' The reedy voice irritated Pearson; he longed to work without interference. He sought for something to heal himself in the garden. He had come to a new post, his first university appointment, thinking to pour the culture and refinement of his mind over his new colleagues. It had been a surprise to him to find thoughts wider and greater than his own, and a wider establishment of learning than he had thought possible in the far-away place he had come to. Every day he had to adjust to some new discovery of his own ignorance. The garden could have been a place for a quiet renewal of his spirit and energy, but it was not so with the presence of the old man.

Eleanor too was strange, she seemed to like Mr Parker so much. Pearson wasted hours waiting for Eleanor, who had slipped down to the shed for two minutes. Sometimes she was there in that biscuit factory, with the stupid old goat, for a whole evening. Really, the old man would have to go. Pearson felt he could not wait to get him away, together with all the rubbish there was down there.

Eleanor said the old man meant well, but Pearson was not so sure of this. He could not understand her attitude, and she was unable to accept what she suddenly saw as a cruel side in his nature.

In the night Eleanor thought she heard a tiny shout. She sat up. Again, a tiny far-away shout in the night.

'It's the old man! Mr Parker's calling us,' she roused Pearson.

'Oh don't fuss,' yawned her husband. 'He's used to being alone. He can look after himself.' He turned over and went on sleeping.

Eleanor went down, in the dark, to the shed. The night was fragrant with the sweet scent of the datura, the long white bells trembled, swinging without noise, and the east wind snored in the restless tree tops. Fantastic firelight danced in the shed and the old man called to her from his dishevelled bed.

'I've got the shivers,' he said. 'There's a good girl! Make up the stove for me and squeeze me some lemons and boil up the kettle.' He gave his orders and his teeth chattered.

'Just a chill,' he comforted Eleanor. 'Get me warm,'

he said, 'an' tomorrer I'll be right you'll see.'

Eleanor did as she was told.

The old man slept a little and Eleanor sat there beside him. In the small light he looked ill and frail. She thought he might die. She thought it would be much easier if he did die. It was not that she wanted him to die, only that if this was the end of his life, and he had lived a long time, it would solve all their difficulties. Lately she had been so unhappy.

'Shall I get the doctor?' she shouted to him when he opened his eyes. But he laughed at her.

'Put some more wood on the stove, my dear. I got the shivers that's all, it's nothing.'

A bit later he opened his eyes.

'Yor husband's a quiet man,' he said. 'Still waters run deep they say.' He gave a little far away laugh, and then he said, 'Thank you, my dear. I'm much obliged to you,' and he slept.

Eleanor went back up the dark garden, the moon rode on the restless fragrance and she felt grateful for the old man's call.

'I think I should sit with him,' she woke Pearson.

'Whatever for, if we weren't here he would be alone.'

'But we are here.' Eleanor stood uneasily by their bed.

'I don't see that that comes into it. We bought the house it's true, and we live in it, but that does not mean we are responsible for the old fool, and his so-called illness.'

'But Pearson, he's really ill.'

'That's his look out. We can't look after all the old

men who are ill. If he doesn't want to be alone, he shouldn't live there. You'll only wear yourself out.' Pearson added his warning.

They seemed to face a wall in their marriage, and they tried to sleep and could not.

By the next weekend Mr Parker was quite recovered.

Pearson was disappointed and angry to see him emerge from the shed as if nothing had been wrong with him. Ignoring advice, 'It's not the best time for it,' Pearson cut dead wood out of the hibiscus. 'Yo'll not touch them roses I hope,' the reedy voice followed Pearson, so he turned his attention to the flame tree. One great bough, he could see, was a danger to the house.

Collecting necessary materials, he set to work. He sat in among the thicket of leaves, straddling a branch near the trunk, and began with his well-cared-for saw to cut the offending limb. Slowly and methodically the saw went to and fro. Pearson was surprised the wood was so soft. He was surprised too at the sharp thorns the tree had all over the branches; from the ground the bark looked quite smooth.

Mr Parker stood under the tree.

'Yo' want to take that branch bit by bit,' he shouted, cupping his mouth with one hand, though Pearson was only a few feet above his head.

'If yo' cut it there it'll tear,' the old man warned. 'Them trees is best cut when the leaves is off.'

'Too heavy,' he explained to Eleanor. 'Too heavy!' he shouted up to Pearson.

'Oh mind your own business you old fool,' Pearson said, but of course Mr Parker was so deaf it didn't matter what anyone said.

Eleanor, standing by, wished Pearson would not look so irritable. There was no pleasure in anything they did now. She smiled at the old man.

'Mr Parker says the branch will tear,' she called up timidly.

'I heard,' Pearson replied grimly, the saw was stuck and he could see he needed something to pull on the branch.

'Throw me the rope,' he called down. Eleanor could pull at the branch from below.

'Yo'll rip right down the trunk,' Mr Parker called. 'He's new to our trees,' he explained to Eleanor.

'Yes, yes, of course,' and she smiled at him.

'Pull! Haul!' Pearson called to Eleanor when the rope was secure.

'What if the branch falls on me?' she cried.

'I'll shout and you run for it,' Pearson called back.

'Pull! Haul!' He saw her straining, but nothing happened. The white smile of wood remained tightly clenched on the saw.

'Yo' need to work at it bit by bit,' Mr Parker said to Eleanor. 'I'm a comin' up!' he called to Pearson. And the next moment he was up the ladder with Pearson's new pruning saw, and off onto the swaying branch along to the end of it, cutting twigs and little branches. Leaf-laden tufts fell to the ground below as he cut this side and that.

'Yo' want to lighten the branch and cut further out to start with,' he explained to Pearson who, red-faced with anger, still sat straddling his branch.

Pearson, before becoming a university professor, had a short but brilliant army career behind him, and he was not going to be ordered about by old men.

'Go down this instant!' he shouted at the old man. His voice was so loud Mr Parker heard it. He stopped his prancing on the branch and stared at Pearson as if unable to understand the reason for the anger.

In that moment Pearson seemed to see the old man as something more than a nuisance; he saw in him something tenacious and evil. And the thought came to him that perhaps many people had taken the house and been forced by reasons, unknown to the land agent, to leave.

'I must be ill,' Pearson thought to himself, 'to have such stupid ideas.' But as he saw Mr Parker coming slowly along the swaying branch he felt he would fight this thing, whatever it was, and he would keep the house; he would fight with all his strength. Mr Parker advanced slowly, in his hand he held the pruning saw and on his face was a strange expression.

From the ground, Eleanor thought he was going to cry, but the awkwardly pointing little saw, with its curve of sharp teeth, frightened her.

'Pearson!' she cried out.

'Go down this instant!' Pearson's voice was deep and loud. And still seated astride the branch, his back against the trunk, he pointed down towards the ground with authority.

'Yo' go down then,' Mr Parker said. In his reedy little voice there was no anger. 'You've more weight nor me. Yo' pull on the rope, an' I'll get her out.' He indicated the saw.

Pearson recognised this as commonsense, but he was not going to be told what to do by this old fool.

'Go down. This instant!' he shouted, still pointing down.

'Well, orl right. I'll have a go on the rope with 'er then.' Mr Parker scrambled down the ladder.

'Come on Missus,' he said to Eleanor, and together they took the rope.

Pearson watched the pantomime below. Eleanor, in her unfashionably long skirt, pulling on the rope with the little old man dangling behind her. The morning had become ridiculous.

'Pull! Haul! Heave! Haul!' he bellowed.

And then, to his amazement, the cut in the branch suddenly widened and, with a roar, the great leaf-laden bough fell away grazing his thigh as it tore down the side of the trunk. He caught the saw before it fell.

'Timbah!' he yelled. 'Run for it!'

Of course Mr Parker heard nothing of the warning. And Eleanor, leaping clear of the heavy falling foliage, tried to grab his shoulder to pull him away, but a forked branch came sharply and painfully between them, and Mr Parker was left there under the heavy fallen mass.

'Oh my God!' Pearson sprang from the tree and pushed through the leaves and branches.

It was an action accompanied by feelings he was

never able to forget afterwards.

Eleanor could only stand and watch. She saw her husband's bare feet, competent and clean in rubber thongs. She thought his feet looked cruel, and she realised they must have always been like that.

Pearson toiled like a sick man to clear out the shed. He cleared and destroyed as if cleaning himself of an infection. The whole place would be different by the time his boys arrived from England.

As he worked he found himself thinking all the time of the old man. He kept expecting to see the washed-out shirt between leaves and bushes, and he missed the persistent reedy voice at his elbow. The garden, so much the old man's place, seemed deserted.

He tried to discipline his mind. He thought about his boys and longed for the time when they would come. He longed for their voices and the noise of their healthy bodies about the house. He wanted to be concerned again with examination results, sports training and dogs and bicycles and the choosing of birthday presents.

The envelope, treasured up all the years, fluttered and fell with the dust being brushed from the beams and rafters. The old man again.

'Who wins a fight anyway,' Pearson muttered to himself. He had to put aside too, the thought that his boys were hardly boys now and would not want the same things from him.

'It's Mr Parker's Valentine.' Eleanor picked it up. 'And he never knew who sent it to him.' She experienced curiosity sadly. Beyond the double doors of the shed, doves laughed softly in the silky morning.

'Put it on the fire,' Pearson ordered.

He thought, as he dragged boxes and tore down ivy, that everything would have been different if the old man had found out all those years ago who had sent him the Valentine.

Eleanor, carrying the dirty envelope up to the house, was thinking the same thing. She had been fondly patient with Mr Parker and knew she was without blame, yet she felt the burden of Pearson's anger and resentment. He had shown how he felt, while she hid her feelings, so giving him full responsibility. She knew they would never speak of any of this now, and she could not reach Pearson in his grim remorse. All day they worked, separately.

'Pearson.' Eleanor called from the house.

'Coming.' He went slowly up the garden.

Some time earlier they had arranged to have a party, a kind of house warming. Neither of them had suggested putting it off. It was time to start preparing for the evening and they tried to smile in readiness for their visitors.

(From *The Travelling Entertainer*, short fiction, 1979.)

CHRIS MCLEOD
WEDDING SUIT

It's like I'm standing in front of a wall of glass; if the glass is broken, if I move ...

But I'm not moving. It's a wall of razors and I'm standing naked. Naked and very still.

I *will* leave her though, one day, soon. I tell this to Helen, but do not mention the wall. A cop-out, she would say. Helen is a practical person, no nonsense. A thing either is or is not. Either I choose her or I choose Jill — it's that simple for Helen.

Choose, Tim, she says, you have to choose.

I see my wife Jill from the back, always the back. If we were to copulate, it would be *a posteriori*, like toads joined in amplexus. But I have not touched her for years now, not really *touched*. We tread carefully, my wife and I, circling, circling.

In bed she wears a yellow tracksuit, terry-towelling; I see her propped on one wide hip. I prop skinny in my grey fleecy-lined tracksuit (it gets cold in the hills where we live). In summer I go to bed with the top off.

We are two wind-socks, drooping on fat pillows.

Jill and I have a daughter, Wendy. Helen says it's a dated name, unfashionable. She has not met Wendy, not yet, but she will like her, of course. Everyone likes little Wendy.

It won't be long now, I tell Helen, but the time must be right.

There won't ever be a right time, Tim, Helen says.

Wendy believes that Banksia Men are bad, like strangers. She worries that one day a Banksia Man will come to our house, even to her room with its pink walls and bright yellow curtains.

Or a stranger will come.

She says she saw a stranger once: an old man who stepped into the road and tried to stop our car. I remember: I swerved to miss him, an old man in a brown suit. He shouted something as we passed. Wendy has not forgotten that old man, from time to time she mentions him.

I don't like strangers, Wendy said then. She was five years old.

I have told Helen it is inevitable that I will leave Jill. *Do* it then, she says.

Always from the back. Jill is in the kitchen, in

front of the window that has the views across the valley. (We chose the house for that window, a long time ago, when such things were important.) Light from the window spreads her, in her yellow tracksuit, like butter. She is washing dishes; detergent bubbles flare and stretch, precarious, like thin safety nets.

But I don't move towards her.

This is not the time or the place.

Helen and I have discussed this, how Jill is to be told. Do it, Helen has said, do it quickly, get it over with. If you really love me you will tell her. It's that simple, Tim.

But I want more time and somehow more honour. The time will present itself, I tell her, I'll know.

Helen wonders *how* I will know. I tell her to be patient.

Anyway, there's Wendy to consider. What's to consider, Helen says — either you want the wife and child package or you want our relationship.

I tell her it's not that simple.

You're copping out, Tim, she says.

In a story that I read to Wendy, a bad Banksia Man was about to drop Snugglepot into a deep, deep hole (things were looking bad), when out sprang the heroic Mr Lizard who engaged the bad Banksia Man in a life or death struggle on a clifftop. The forces of good, as represented by Mr Lizard, were to triumph on this occasion and the bad Banksia Man was rendered deadibones.

Wendy repeated the word with some satisfaction: Deadibones, she said.

It was the way things were meant to be, a resolution with hope and honour.

Helen is younger than me and has no children. She is the French teacher at the school where I also teach.

That is something that Jill and I may have laughed at once: running off with the French mistress — it sounds like the plot of a foolish and cheap romance. Perhaps it is.

We don't laugh much now though. But we are loving parents. Maybe that's enough, I don't know. I'm standing in front of my glass wall and I don't know. Helen says that I don't want to make a decision, that I want the best of both worlds.

More time, I tell her. I want more time, that's all.

Sometimes Helen seems almost callous — there's more to consider here than just our needs. What about my daughter? Helen says that leaving Jill and leaving Wendy are not the same thing — I will still have my daughter, the relationship will continue.

But she doesn't know Jill.

She's right though, I'm sure. Things will work out, with honour. And I do want Helen, of course I do; she *sees* me, she *touches* me.

Jill and I are with friends, Peter and Clare. Peter is a lawyer who also plays the piano and has affairs (he has other interests, but pursues them with less diligence). I have known him since university; it is our friendship that has brought our wives together. He has told me that Clare doesn't know about his affairs; they are unimportant anyway. He says she doesn't need to know. They have a daughter, Megan, who is Wendy's age.

The two girls are together in Megan's room. Peter is playing some Chopin. Jill and Clare are listening, sitting together on a sofa. Jill's heavy skirt has fallen slightly away from the back of her legs, revealing a navy-blue slip with a lace trim.

It looks foolish and matronly. I didn't know that she owned such a garment. She isn't someone I know any more.

I watch Clare watching Peter and wonder if she knows him.

Later, Jill says to me that Peter has such talent; it's a shame that he hasn't been able to go further with his music.

I tell her that he hasn't wanted to, it's only an interest, something on the side.

Such a shame, she says.

Jill says that I'm not *there* for her any more.

I shrug.

Is it something we should talk about? she says.

No, I say.

What's the matter then?

Nothing.

Jill turns her wide hips, her mother's hips. She walks out of the room. I'm not completely stupid, Tim, she says over her shoulder.

My friend Peter tells me that a bit on the side is all right, but not worth breaking up a family for. The family, he says, that's the important thing. Look, he says, you've built this thing with Jill, you have Wendy, you have the house. Why jeopardise all that?

There's nothing left with Jill, I tell him. Really, there's only Wendy in common now.

So? he says.

It's not enough.

Don't be stupid, mate, Peter tells me. Don't be bloody stupid, she'd screw you for every cent you've got. I see it every day of the week.

It's happened a few times now, in the middle of the night. I'm fast asleep and Jill starts hitting me. She seems to be doing it in her sleep, but I don't know.

The next morning she can never remember it happening.

Otherwise, things go on as normal between us: we wear our tracksuits, we circle one another.

Helen doesn't understand my feelings for Wendy. How can she? — she hasn't had children of her own.

One day though I'm sure she'll love Wendy as I do. She's a beautiful little girl. Sometimes I fantasise the three of us together; it's a warm, slow picture.

Helen says she isn't going to wait forever.

Wendy says, You know the man we saw, Daddy, the stranger? Well, I was thinking about his suit.

What about it? I ask.

They all have suits, don't they?

Who, Wendy?

Men, like that, old men. You see them from the car. Do they wear their wedding suit?

What do you mean?

The suit you wear when you get married, if you're a man. Men keep them, don't they?

I don't tell her, but I know: they keep them until they run naked at a glass wall, a razor wall.

Thick, wind-proof wedding suits.

(From *Homing*, short fiction, 1990.)

LIZ BYRSKI
THIRTY-SEVEN YEARS

'Is he going to call again?' asks my son Neil the next day.

'He already called again this morning,' my friend Irene tells him. 'Before you were awake — that's three times in less than twelve hours.'

They stand looking at me and fleetingly I feel that I am back in the kitchen at Smugglers Cottage with my mother questioning me about kissing in the pub.

'So,' says Neil. 'What next?'

'I don't know. I just don't know.'

'You could go to San Francisco and see him!'

'He says he'll come to Perth.'

'You should go there, it's the adventure you need.'

'I don't know.'

'Whoops! Sorry!' says Irene racing to the compact disc player as Nat King Cole launches into 'Too Young' and tears run down my cheeks. She whips

Nat back into his case and puts on a Beethoven piano concerto unaware of its even greater poignancy.

'How do you feel?'

I shake my head and gaze out onto the windswept fields at the back of the house; fields where I had so often walked with him; where we had kissed under the oak trees, their branches as bare then as now.

'How strange that I was here, when he found me. It's only the second time I've been back to England in eighteen years. I wouldn't dare put it in a book, no one would believe the coincidence.'

Irene wraps the break and puts it away. She wipes the worktop and shakes crumbs into the bin.

'Perhaps it's not coincidence, perhaps it's fate.'

She surprises me, Irene is not given to conversations about fate. She's a realist and a sceptic, a business woman, independent, strong minded and down to earth. 'He called last week and again before you arrived, he sounds delightful, he thought you might not speak to him. How do you feel?'

'I don't know.'

We decide to go to Brighton and Neil takes the road past Three Bridges Station.

'This was where I last saw him, where we said goodbye.'

To Neil it is only of passing interest as he negotiates the traffic. To me it is re-enactment. Thirty-seven years ago his eyes burned black with sadness as he walked away from me here and I never saw him again.

'Do you actually want someone in your life?' Neil asks. 'You like being single, it suits you. You've been very clear about that.'

'Yesterday I was very clear about it. I didn't want anyone. I wanted to be alone. But this is different.'

'So what do you want?'

'I don't know.'

I know nothing. I am numb with shock. Thrilled? Excited? Confused? Terrified? What if I let myself feel again? What if instead of just looking at those jewels of memory I let myself wear them? I have grown so good at defence, will I protect myself now, or will I open it all up again? Will I declare myself or wait in the tension to see what happens? I will wait, I have to, I'm incapable of anything else at present.

'I want you to understand,' Karl says, 'that I don't expect anything. I just had to find you, to explain, to tell you how sorry I am for my stupidity.' He pauses. I can hear his breathing, he swallows hard. 'I wanted to tell you that I really loved you, that you were the love of my life and I was never able to forget. I always loved you, I still love you.'

I dare not answer. I cannot tell him what I feel because I am so frozen with shock. All these years I knew how I loved him, now I am incapable of saying so; incapable of feeling anything, paralysed by the fear of the consequences of speaking it, stunned by his frankness and by the feeling that nothing — absolutely nothing — has changed but everything is different.

The next day, Tuesday, flowers arrive, masses

of flowers. It takes two people to carry them in: orchids and lilies, carnations, roses and tulips; pink, white, cream, lemon, mauve and the palest green.

'Good heavens,' says Irene. 'I've never seen anything like it. I don't have enough vases.'

'We couldn't actually get any more flowers in the van,' says the florist climbing back into it.

We search cupboards and the loft for vases and pots which we fill and carry into every room. The house is like a diva's dressing room on opening night.

'I wanted a sea of flowers to be waiting for you when you arrived,' he explains. 'A sea of flowers with my card on them. I thought they might persuade you to speak to me when I called, but no one would deliver on Boxing Day or on Monday.'

'They're so beautiful,' I say. 'So beautiful, thank you.'

'I hope they tell you something. I don't have the words.'

And still the great block of frozen tears remains cold and heavy inside, protecting me. While it is there I am safe, I can turn and walk away, I can put down the phone. I can pack my bags, go home to Australia and pretend this never happened, everything will be just as it was before, safe, manageable, intact.

On Wednesday morning at seven o'clock the telephone rings. Irene has gone back to work after the Christmas break. Neil has gone to London. Still half asleep I run downstairs in the dark to answer it. I wrap a blanket around my shoulders and sit on the floor in the hall.

'I loved it so much when you played the piano for me,' I say.

'Really,' he says. 'I never knew, you never said anything.'

I am shocked to discover that I never let him know what I felt when he played to me, how it thrilled me to see his hands on the keys, to hear the music he made. Perhaps there are other things I never told him. Did I ever really let him know how much I loved him? Did all that coaching in ladylike restraint hold me back from an honest declaration of all that I felt? Perhaps.

'Do you remember playing "Wooden Heart"?'

'"*Muss i denn*"? Yes I remember:

Muss i denn, muss i denn,
Zum Staedtele hinaus,
staedtele hinaus,
und Du mein Schatz bleibst hier.'

'That song is in my heart for you, always, always,' I say.

'Sweetheart!' he says and with that one word the ice shatters. I am eighteen again, I am back in the park at Northumberland Crescent, back by the lake, back on his bed in Bobby's house, and in Smugglers Cottage. I am back again to a wet July morning with the rain smudging the words from the pages of his letter and my life disintegrating before my eyes. He has broken into my heart, stripped away my defences and forced me into my feelings. Even the illusion of safety is gone and through my tears I tell him what I should have told him on the telephone thirty-seven years earlier.

'I love you. I've always loved you. It was always you.'

***

Twice a day he calls. Twice a day we talk for hours as the San Francisco telephone company counts its blessings and offers him a special rate for calls to England. Twice a day we sway joyfully, perilously back and forth across the miles, across the years. We fill in the blanks of memory, breach the gaps of time. We piece together the past we share, we share the past we lost. Our conversations are rich with rediscovery, frustrated by memory, woven through with regret.

'The Prospect of Whitby,' he says. 'That was the most important night of my life.'

'The what?'

'The Prospect of Whitby. The pub — the pub where we first kissed.'

'Is that where we went that night?'

'Yes — the pub, down in the docks, the Prospect of Whitby! You can't have forgotten.'

I admit to the black hole in my memory that lasts from the moment he came into the house and is not restored until we are sitting in the kitchen supervised by Jock.

He is devastated. It is as though I've smashed his most treasured possession. I have lost his most precious memory. There is an edge to his voice, he almost believes it's deliberate and I know I've hurt him immeasurably.

'Perhaps you forgot because it meant nothing.'

'It's not like that.'

'Perhaps you were so used to being kissed in pubs.'

'Look, I know it can have been neither of those things. It's not that I just forgot, it's something more — the whole evening has gone.'

He can't let it go. He can't laugh it off or shrug it away with regret. He is wounded and I am reminded of his extreme sensitivity, how intensely he feels things, how quick he is to attribute his own meaning to words and events. I'm fearful of his need for the past to be as he remembers it, for me to be as he has made me in his heart. And try as I do I can't remember the Prospect of Whitby. As we talk each of us reminds the other of forgotten incidents, the memories are restored, the moments flash back and are revived, but for me the Prospect of Whitby remains a blank sheet. It is the first moment of tension between us, a wisp of dark cloud drifting across the face of the sun. There will be others, some will drift back and forth, while others evaporate in the warmth of the sun's rays.

'You were so honourable,' I say. 'I've always cherished the fact that you protected my innocence.'

'I've wondered if you thought me a fool,' he says. 'But I promised your father.'

'Promised my father? Promised him what? When?'

'That first weekend I came to stay.'

'What did you promise?'

'That we wouldn't have intimate relations.'

'Why? Why did you promise that? Did you two talk about me that first weekend?'

'Of course — he was worried because I was so much older, he wanted to preserve your virginity.'

I am shocked, affronted. Thirty-seven years have passed and I react to the news with the indignation of a woman in her fifties who has spent the last twenty years writing about the rights of women to control their bodies and their lives. I can see them walking side by side together in the garden as they did that weekend, heads bent close in conversation — or was it conspiracy? Men's business, too serious to be interrupted by or shared with women. They were talking about me, as though I was a child or a piece of property. They were deciding what would happen to me, how I would be managed and I wasn't even consulted.

'Your father was trying to protect you,' he says. 'And I loved you and respected you. Your innocence was precious and I respected your father too. He wanted the best for you. I assumed you knew about this, that he'd spoken to you and you'd agreed to it too. You said just now that you cherished the fact that I didn't make love to you.'

'But I thought that was your choice, not my father's.'

'He loved you, he wanted—'

'He wanted to dictate what happened to me, what happened between us.'

'And was that so wrong? You can't blame him

for wanting to protect you. Haven't you had those feelings about your own children? Don't you still want to protect them?'

'Yes — but the thing is that you two had this conversation without me — behind my back.'

'Well we could hardly have had it in front of you. This was nineteen sixty-two — it's unthinkable that the three of us would have discussed it together, that's how it was then. If it had been my daughter I would have done the same thing.'

I try to unravel my anger, questioning whether or not it makes any sense. Is it relevant? Is this a political reaction to a personal experience? But isn't the personal political? Isn't that the core of feminist thought?

'I don't understand,' he says, cautious now. 'I wanted to care for you. I had to go back to America — suppose I had died before we married, wasn't it important that you retained your innocence?'

'I suppose so — yes, it was in those days, but that should have been for me to decide. I thought you took control because it was what you thought was right.'

'So did I. But without the promise to your father I might well have weakened.'

There is a pause as we both remember the day in Bobby's house and all the other occasions on which we came so close to breaking the promise.

'I know you would have allowed it,' he says softly, almost shyly.

'Yes.'

'I knew it was my responsibility.'

I am locked in silent battle with my feelings.

'If you had known then,' he asks, 'about our conversation, about your father's request, would you have felt angry or insulted?'

I want to say yes. I want to say I was always a feminist at heart, that those things were always important to me — but I can't and I have to struggle to tell the truth and not to rewrite the past as I want it to be.

'No,' I admit slowly. 'I think I might have felt embarrassed that you were talking about me but I wouldn't have been able to define it. And yes, I guess I would have accepted that that was how things were done. I couldn't have put it in the broader context in which I see it now.'

'So does it matter thirty-seven years later? Does it matter to you and me now?'

I know this question is crucial. It's about separating the past from the present, about who I was at eighteen and the world I lived in then and who I am at fifty-four, and the knowledge I have gained and the views I have formed in the intervening years. This is the challenge in matching the two selves, in interpreting the past and living the present. This is the challenge of ideology versus the reality of experience. What does she really feel, this woman that I have become? How much of what I have written and spoken in my public life have I integrated? How much is rhetoric and how much is feeling? Will I allow theory to dominate or capitulate to instinct and feeling?

'I think it doesn't matter,' I begin. 'I think that I'm confusing the way I was then, with how I would feel now. In those days I was happy for you to take control of everything. All I wanted was to marry you and the girl or woman I was then wouldn't have questioned anything you said. I was very submissive — I was happy to do as you said.' I pause and he waits in the silence for me to continue.

'What matters is the love and respect you showed me, and indeed my father. What matters is the sort of person you were and what motivated you. That's what's important.'

'The fact that you were so submissive placed a special responsibility on me,' he says. 'A special responsibility not to abuse your trust.' Now he, in turn pauses, gathering his thoughts.

'I was in a kind of madness in my possessiveness. When I got your letters I was terrified of you needing other men. I'm not sure if you understand the emotional power you had over me. After Melanie — well I couldn't face that again. I truly felt I could not survive it. There was another architect in the office whose younger wife had just left him for someone else. It destroyed him. He was incapable of working; he would sit every day at his drawing board gazing into space, unable to live any sort of life and he became a shell of a man. I knew that could happen to me and I had developed a sort of emotional radar so sensitive it could detect a mosquito flying over Siberia — you had that power over me and I had to escape.'

The enormity of the things we were unable to tell each other at the time astounds me. The vulnerability we had both felt, never fully expressed. How different it might have been had we both felt safe to reveal the full extent of our fears and our feelings for each other. Years before 'dependence' became part of the popular jargon to define 'unhealthy' relationships we had censored the expression of our need and dependence in order to protect ourselves and preserve our foolish pride.

I take a deep breath and ask him the question I have so often asked myself.

'I understand how vulnerable you were,' I say. 'But what would have happened if you had broken that promise — if we had slept together?'

He pauses for what seems a long time and I can hear him struggling to gain control of his voice.

'Don't you see,' he says, softly. 'If we had slept together I could never have left you. I would have felt a moral obligation to return to England and marry you. I could not have walked away. Now do you still admire me for taking control? Are you still glad that I didn't make love to you?'

I see thirty-seven lost years. Years lost for so many reasons; interference by other people, prejudice, misunderstanding, immaturity, pride, good intentions and fear — most of all fear — my parents' fear, Karl's fear, my own fear. I admire and cherish his honourable restraint as an expression of his love, but part of me chafes at the knowledge that it is sexual possession that could have brought him back. The message is as old as time. It is about ownership. What will feminist theory do with this one?

Slowly, lovingly, sometimes painfully the layers are peeled away, the gaps are filled, the perceptions exchanged; confusion moves to clarity; anxiety is replaced with confidence. And through it all shines the brave and beautiful truth that for thirty-seven years he has loved me, and he had the courage and the commitment to find me and to step back into my life.

A week has passed since he first called. It is a week that has changed my life, changed the past, changed the present: but what does it mean for the future? In another week I will go back to Lisbon, and ten days later return to Australia. I will go back to the life I made for myself, back to my hard won solitude, back to my safe house, to my work, my friends, my dog, but I know that these clothes of my old life no longer fit. For I am changed, totally and completely changed and although I can't yet define that change I know it is fundamental. I don't want to leave England, here in the places he knows, in the places we were together I feel close to him. I'm frightened to leave, frightened to burst the bubble, frightened that when I step off the plane in Perth this magic will disappear on a hot summer breeze and it will all be over. Once again he will be gone, leaving a great void in my life, a loss so great it cannot be repaired.

What does this all mean? I walk the boundaries of a fantasy future in which we are together, beginning now the life we should have shared years ago. But I dare not venture into the centre of this particular emotional whirlpool.

During our first conversation he had told me he wanted to see me and I dream of meeting his flight, driving him home to Fremantle and watching him move around my house. I know he will love the angles, the space, the rammed earth walls and the rich tones of the jarrah, the sunlight splashing through the big windows, the harmony of colours and textures, the sunlit deck and the small garden with its iceberg roses, lavender and citrus trees. I dream of swimming with him in the early mornings off South Beach, and walking there hand in hand as the sun sets and steals away the daylight. I picture sitting with him at a cafe on the cappuccino strip, introducing him to friends, shopping in the markets, cooking a meal together, sharing breakfast with him on the deck in the early morning. I dream of leading him through the damp green forests and vineyards of the south west, and the endless white dunes of the southern coast.

But most of all I dream of the way he was and the way he now might be. I dream of the tenderness of his touch and the sweetness of his smile, and the way the hard edge of his voice softened when he spoke to me, and of how he kissed me and touched my face and told me he loved me all those years ago. Through those dreams a thread of fear weaves back and forth, it questions whether he will still love me in Australia as he had in England and in memory, or whether he is just in love with a dream that he had thought was lost forever.

'Perhaps I could come to Lisbon,' he says. 'Perhaps we could meet before you go back to Australia?'

'Not Lisbon,' I reply, knowing that there I will have to divide my attention and my energy between him and Neil. Knowing that the best place is one where we can be alone.

'But my ticket takes me through a stop in Frankfurt on the way home to Perth.'

'I'll fly to Frankfurt,' he says without hesitation. 'Will you meet me in Frankfurt?'

(From *Remember Me*, a memoir, 2000.)

IRIS LAVELL
UNDER THE CIRCUMSTANCES

The opportunity more or less falls into their laps. Gordon has had to fly back to Scotland because his mother is ill, so Harry has arranged to meet Carole at her place. When he gets there she takes a while to answer the bell.

'Who is it?' she eventually asks through the closed door.

'It's me, Harry,' he says, feeling foolish. Who did she think it was?

She opens the door. She is wearing a pair of dark blue pyjamas made out of some sort of silky material. Her hair, which she normally keeps tied up, is hanging loose. She looks younger, more approachable, less businesslike than normal.

'Oh Harry,' she says, 'just making sure. There's something wrong with the peephole. Come on through.'

She is wearing a familiar perfume. Harry has a flashback — Yasamine dressed in a smooth black dress. She was wearing the locket he gave her for her birthday. He just fastened the clasp of the chain, and his fingers stopped to play with the fine silk of her skin. He wound his arms around her from behind and buried his face in her hair. He feels the sensation of it now on his cheeks. He shakes the thought away. He is here, now, in Carole's house, and not with his ex-wife.

He is more nervous than he had expected. It's not the first time he's done something like this, but he hasn't been with anyone else since he moved in with Louisa, and her best friend is high stakes. The foreplay is over. This is the real deal.

He smiles, raises his eyebrows, and hands her the flowers he's bought from a roadside stall that is permanently set up around the corner from his house. The flower-seller is surly and never says more than two words, so there's no chance of it getting back to Louisa. If it did he'd say they were for his mother. The flowers are all pungent smells and bright colours, and the oversized bunch is wrapped in purple and red paper. One orange daisy thing is hanging its head as if its neck is broken.

Carole relieves him of the flowers and puts them on the hall stand beneath the pictures of her grandchildren.

'How thoughtful.'

She kisses his cheek, lingering there and slowly working her way around to his ear. Her perfume is heavy but not suffocating. His ear is cold where she has licked it. When she turns to get him a drink, his hand automatically goes up to wipe his cheek.

'Here's something I prepared earlier,' she says, handing him the drink.

'Thanks.'

'Don't mention it,' she says. She leads him into the sitting room and sits on the couch. 'Come and sit down.' She pats the seat next to her.

Harry sits, takes the glass from her hand and puts it on the table at his side, slopping a little over the rim and his hand as he does so. Carole takes his hand and licks the spilt drink from his fingers. It feels strange and Harry has the urge to laugh, but he controls himself.

'Sweet,' she says. 'Intoxicating.' She is leaning over him. He can see down her pyjama top. Her nipples are erect. He feels himself getting hard. It feels good to be hot, and he finds it reassuring that he is responding as easily as he is.

'Keep it up,' he says, half to himself.

'Couldn't have put it better myself,' says Carole. 'I'd better wipe that up off the table before it marks,' she says, grabbing a handful of tissues.

'Sorry,' he says.

'Don't worry about it.' She mops it up, leaning over him. Her pyjamas are silk and slide around on her body without making sparks: none of that cheap polyester stuff that Louisa wears. 'I don't want you to worry one bit,' she says.

'I wasn't,' he says, taking her wrist. He kisses her, a long, deep, slow kiss. She has just cleaned her teeth and is wearing some sort of flavoured lipstick. 'You taste nice,' he says.

'So do you.' She pushes him down so that he is only half lying on the couch, with his legs angled down to the floor, and climbs on top of him. 'I like it on top,' she says. 'I like to feel strong and powerful. I like to take control. All you need to do is what I tell you to.'

'Great,' he says. 'I like a woman who knows her own mind.'

She unties her complicated pyjama top without Harry seeing how. She has the body of a younger woman, at variance with her face. Harry vaguely wonders if she's had some sort of cosmetic surgery. Gordon has plenty of money and is generous enough, he thinks, and Carole's got a good job too. Between the two of them they'd be doing all right.

Carole starts to undo his shirt, kissing his neck and his chest as she goes down on his body. 'Mm, nice chest,' she says. 'What else do we have down here? What's this here?'

'I think that's pretty obvious,' he says. He cups his hands over her breasts, but the position is awkward and he lets go. She goes down on him now, licking and sucking.

He is uncomfortable, not enjoying it as much as he should. He clears his throat. 'Do you have a bed?' he says after a moment. 'It's just that my back is killing me.'

'Oh come on,' says Carole. 'Don't be an old man.'

She keeps playing with him, kissing him, teasing him with her tongue.

'Well as far as that goes you're hardly sixteen yourself, are you?' Harry snaps this more than he intends to. His back has started to hurt quite badly and the pain is shooting down his left leg.

She stops and sits up. He adjusts his position and the pain subsides a bit.

'What?' she says.

'You're not, are you?' he says, still irritably adjusting his position underneath her. 'Anyway that's what beds are for. More room to manoeuvre.' He winks at her to relieve the tension.

Carole recoils slightly. She is reconsidering. 'It's upstairs,' she says, but there is an edge to her voice now. Then she laughs. 'Sometimes I forget,' she says as she climbs off him and stands up. 'You're right. We're not as young as we used to be. Gordon prefers the bed too. Come on.'

'You're only as young as the woman you feel,' says Harry automatically. He uses this line with Louisa all the time and she always smiles, but Carole doesn't get the joke. Too bad! He is annoyed that she has brought Gordon into the picture. There should be some sort of unspoken rule about that.

He is still lying halfway off the couch and he asks her for some help to get up. She grabs hold of his arms and pulls him sharply.

'Ow! Take it easy.' His erection has fallen away completely. Bugger. He's not as reliable as he used to be, but it's understandable under the circumstances.

'Sorry,' she says. She sounds resentful, petulant, childish.

'It's okay. I'll do it myself.' He eases himself off the couch until he twists around onto his knees, and leans forwards into the seat-back. He stays there a while, head down, backside facing outwards.

'Nice,' says Carole.

She doesn't stay to watch, or to help further. She clears the glasses and Harry hears her rinse them and put them in the dishwasher. When she comes back into the room, he has made it to his feet but is having difficulty straightening up.

'I need a moment,' he says.

'How do you feel about this?' She has tied her hair up.

'Not great,' he says.

'Me neither,' she says.

'I think I've put my back out. Can I take a raincheck? To tell the truth I haven't been feeling the best lately.'

'I'll have to get back to you on that.'

'Well,' he says.

'Well.'

'I'll see myself out then,' he says.

'Suit yourself.'

Okay, thinks Harry, I will.

'We'll catch up,' he offers. 'Soon.'

'Of course. Give Louisa my love.'

'Very funny.'

As he drives home he is feeling humiliated and annoyed with himself. What was he thinking? She's hardly his type: all feminist hard edges and neurosis. He knows, he knows from past experience that there is a reason why people don't sleep with their wives' friends or with workmates. You have to keep seeing them, and maintaining a pretended innocence. It's all so exhausting and, besides, he's not a hundred per cent convinced that he can trust Carole not to tell Gordon, or Louisa for that matter.

Plus he likes Gordon, he really does, and he doesn't want to lose their recently burgeoning friendship. He doesn't like to think how finding out about this would hurt and humiliate him, and for what? He feels like an idiot. He'll kick himself if he loses Gordon's good opinion. These days, friends are few and far between.

Louisa isn't in when he gets home but the dog greets him, sniffs at his groin then wanders out the back. 'Oh, come on!' he protests. 'Et tu, Buster?'

But it's fair comment. Before Louisa gets home he will have a shower and pop his clothes in the wash. Just to be on the safe side.

(From *Elsewhere in Success*, a novel, 2013.)

JOAN LONDON
ENOUGH ROPE

Every now and then an energy builds up in me and I know that it's time to visit Michael. Quite suddenly everything, the set of rooms I move through, the seesaw glare and darkness as I pass outside and in, the glint of the dam down on the boundary, becomes the background to a dream.

I rush the boys off to the school-bus and throw my packed bag into the car. Ian just watches me. But we've finished seeding and I haven't visited my mother for a long time.

At the first roadhouse in the metropolitan area I ring Michael at the school where he is teaching.

'Oh hello,' he says. I can hear the faint, endless barracking of children in a playground. 'Tonight? Yes, fine, see you then.' He could be making an appointment with an anxious parent.

I always arrive rather windswept on Michael's doorstep. This is a tradition. It is not windy on the quiet streets of Lakeside Estate where Michael has lived since his marriage. But he used to live on the top floor of a block of flats with a cosmopolitan's-eye view of Perth. In those days, when the boys were very young, I was always late. I would stand for a moment in the cold tunnels of city air and study the careful schoolteacher script of *M. Makevis* beside the door.

I still wear an air of haste and escape now, dodging among the hanging baskets on Michael's discreet front porch. It is a form of apology. I juggle with my bottles in their damp paper sleeves — beer, wine or champagne, I try to vary them so as not to look too predictable.

'Bon soir,' says Michael, while his door-chimes are still pealing. This greeting is again a tradition. Years ago at teachers' college, we liked to season our exchanges with 'adieu' and 'merci bien' and 'c'est pas mal tu sais'. Unlike the French however, we do not kiss on meeting. It leaves, has always left, a tiny gap, during which Michael takes my bottles into the kitchen and I try to decide where to sit.

There is something deliberate about Michael's clatter in the kitchen.

'Is Lauren home?' I call across the bar.

'She's rehearsing.' He brings in our drinks. 'She's got a recital next week.'

She wasn't home the last time I visited either.

'Your house is looking great,' I say, though in this

dimmed light I can't notice any change. Couches seem to grow out of the pale carpet. The smoky glass of the coffee table is still unsmudged and bare. It stretches between us, shin to shin. His are crossed, in pale jeans.

'We finished the music room last week.' He puts down his drink. 'Would you like to have a look?'

For the first time he leads me into the private part of his house. An old sensation of conspiracy unfolds as I follow him down a corridor. We used to stifle laughter in my mother's kitchen once, making coffee late at night. Something about the cannisters' diminuendo from big FLOUR to little TEA ...

'... but the view'll improve when the trees have grown,' he is saying. We are crossing a little courtyard. I glimpse a plastic washing basket, an upturned mop, ordinary domesticity. 'She always hated me listening when she practised.' He smiles at this over his shoulder as he unlocks the door.

The music room smells new, of pine and cement. Lauren's baby grand stands sleek and black in the middle of the room. There is an old couch under a bare window. Michael stays by the door.

'I bet Lauren's in here all the time,' I say, opening the piano.

'Not a great deal yet.' His hand is on the light switch, ready to go. 'She's very involved with this Bach group. Out nearly every night. Though she's got a friend, a flautist, who comes over in the day sometimes to play duets.'

He locks the door again as we go out.

'How are the boys?'

This is better. We are on sure ground here. For Michael this is no routine enquiry. They are restless, I say, and too rough with each other at the moment. Ian says they need pulling into line. My voice is hesitant. I think they're bored at school.

Michael nods. He starts talking about his class. The theme this term is the planets: the space-ship they're building is becoming more complex than he can always understand. It incorporates the school computer. The boys in his class are working really well together since they started this project.

I say I do not think Miss MacPherson at the Yardoo Primary goes in for the space age. 'I wish *you* taught the boys.' I think I say this every time I see him. And he just gives the same half smile and goes on talking. Of course. Even as a student Michael had his own ideas. I listened, but ended up going with the stream: *don't let the little bastards get you down*.

I think about the time I brought the boys here to see Michael. As usual we were staying with my mother.

'You certainly have your hands full,' my mother always says.

Michael had taped the World Cup soccer final ready for them on his video. He showed them how to make a milkshake.

'Wow this place is like that T.V. commercial,' I heard them tell him in the kitchen. They swivelled on his bar-stools and tried their jokes on him.

'Can we go to Michael's?' they still ask me when we're driving to the city.

Michael is still talking. This year he has been posted to a school in a wealthy middle-class area. The kids are great — Michael always says this about his classes, they're *his* kids now — but there are different sorts of problems. Some of the parents push their children, ask Michael when he'll be giving the class real work to do.

'Have I told you this already?'

'No no, go on.' I can watch him as I used to when he talked. In winter his face is so pale it's almost luminous. 'Milkface': that's what the kids called him when he first came to Australia. He stood on the edge of the playground in the shorts made by his mother and saw that no one else wore shorts below the knee. He told me that once.

'Things are changing,' he is saying. 'I think the children are the only ones who can keep up.' Now he's cupped his palm and balanced his empty glass on it. 'But you have to trust them, you have to let them go a bit ...' He flicks his glass with his other hand and strikes a precarious note.

Michael and Lauren have no children. This has never surprised me although they've been married for some years. Perhaps it's because I always think of Lauren as being very young. She must be in her late twenties now, but the last time I saw her she was as thin and childlike as ever. She has a little flat white face, with eyes and nose and mouth crowded together, and a bush of crinkly brown hair springing back from her forehead.

I couldn't say that I really know Lauren. When

Michael wrote to tell me he was married, I arrived at the new house with champagne and a wedding present. Michael met me juggling a glass of dissolving disprin. Lauren had a headache, she was going to bed. She sat in a dressing-gown on the arm of his chair while he opened the present.

'Thanks very much,' she said as she got up to leave.

She was very gifted, Michael explained in a low voice. Her mother had pushed her, practice six hours a day, no friends, talent quests, frilly dresses. It was amazing she still wanted to play at all. She was very strong really, knew what she wanted. He was helping her work towards that.

Yes, I'd said then, looking around me. Lakeside Estate. Full-page, colour supplement, *Where your dreams become realities*. We drank a toast to his marriage, smiling but not finding much to say.

I've never told Michael about the time I saw him and Lauren at the lake. We were down for the Show, I'd taken the boys there to let off steam. They disappeared, I sat in the car to look at people. It was a wet and windy Sunday afternoon. Some sort of a club, or an office on picnic, was playing a rather bossy game of cricket with an outfield of girlfriends slouching among the eskies. I saw them suddenly, weaving their way through the players. Their familiarity, Michael's leather jacket, Lauren's hunched shoulders and blowing woolly hair, materialised for me as if I'd been expecting them.

I saw Lauren break away, veer towards the lake, stand looking down with her hands in the pockets of her parka. Michael followed, said something to her, set off towards the kiosk. He walked right near my car on his way back to her. I saw that he was holding two icecreams. His head was bent and he had a little smile on his face. You've got your hands full Michael, I caught myself thinking.

Tonight Michael and I are shifting fast from second gear into third. We haven't got this far past the rituals for a long time. Michael's given up on getting drinks for us from his bar. He's put a flagon of wine and the whisky bottle on the table between us. Through it I discover an aquarium view of my blind stockinged feet.

Better make this my last, I think into my wine. Or second last. But already I'm feeling that gathering of cheer that means it could be too late for limits. Recently I've been rather pushing the limits, all around the district. *You* certainly enjoyed yourself, people tell me later. The end of every social occasion has been a blank. When I come to, I'm alone in a quietly throbbing car. Ian is outside, opening our gate in the moonlight. He gets back in the car, I shut my eyes, the car lurches forward, then throbs to itself again. I open my eyes. Ian is closing the gate. Limits.

I don't want Michael to know this. I don't want him to have to escort me reeling to the car. Or worse. Throwing up into his native garden. There's a lot I don't want him to know about me. My triviality. My laziness. How much I weigh. Our relationship, as I've often told myself, is characterised by a beautiful restraint.

Although tonight Michael himself is not holding back, I notice. As he leans forward to pour himself another whisky, a strand of hair falls across his forehead. He leaves it there. He rips open a packet of peanuts and makes an avalanche of them into a bowl. Both of us laddle up peanuts and munch in an absent-minded way.

'You know Michael,' I say, 'there isn't one sign of Lauren in this room.'

He looks at me.

'Ah yes.' My remark hangs between us. 'Ah yes. My waiting room.'

'Oh I don't mean ...'

'My waiting room. Where I *wait*.' There's that little smile again that creases up his eyes.

'Lauren's rehearsing ...'

'Ah yes.'

I don't recognise the new cut of his tone. It goes with the smile. '*And* Lauren cannot drive. Therefore the flautist must give her a lift. The Polish flautist.'

This time I say nothing.

'And I wait.' He says this to me as if I might accuse him of something.

Michael and I can't sit and face each other any more. Michael has wandered off somewhere. But first he's put on some soft jazz, as if to keep me company.

I'm sorry, I say across this room where I don't belong. I've never known what Michael wanted of me. Even if that meant keeping away.

What now? I lean back, shut my eyes, waiting. But

my centre of gravity seems to have moved to my left ear. I slide my cheek down into the rough surface of Michael's couch. With one eye I survey a tweed horizon. I see the colours of the native garden growing across this suburban block. Grey sand laps the feet of a raw brown fence. Dull green nursery saplings shake their name-tags beside gravel paths. He says their names to himself as he passes. One day they will wave a private shelter around his house, her music room.

How do I know about waiting?

Once Michael and I sat in a cafe, saying goodbye. We had both just graduated. Michael was leaving for Europe the next day. I didn't know where I was going.

It was January, but it had been a day of freak tropical rain. Cars swished by outside in a luxuriant greenish twilight. The jukebox was playing bouzouki music, the cafe-owner smiled at us. We'd often sat here, it was one of the few places in this city with any atmosphere, we said. But this time Michael kept checking his watch. He showed me his ticket and stowed it away again with careful fingers.

'I'd better get you home. I'd better get myself home. My last night and all that.' He smiled at me for our old shared bondage. I did not respond. Our widowed mothers sat on opposite sides of the city. His mother wore black, served sweet black coffee in tiny cups, spoke in another language. But about the same things, Michael said. Probed and warned, chased up lineages. We had been encircled. But he was getting away.

I couldn't look at him. This new, harder presence, no longer attending me, was suddenly proof of its own value. I felt him at the edge of my shoulder, at the tips of my fingers, at arm's length where I had been so careful to keep him. Quiet, pale Michael Makevis.

'Wait!' I said outside the cafe. I was scrabbling in strange desperation for my sunglasses. It had stopped raining, the footpath glared, the air was again thin and bright.

The hallway at home was stuffy.

'That you love?' I chose not to answer. I could still hear his car at the end of our road.

'Let-ter!' She must be lying down because of the heat … There was a manila envelope waiting for me under the jardiniere. O.H.M.S. My posting had come. Grades 3 and 4, Yardoo Primary.

It is raining now, steady winter rain beating on the hollow of Michael's house. The sound has been creeping up on me ever since the music died. The button glows red on the stereo. Salt dribbles from the empty peanut packet onto the glass table. No Michael.

I leap up from the couch, and hobbling on my numbed left foot as if I'm tethered, open the front door. My car still sits askew on the verge, its wheels streaked with wet country dust. The air is very cold. Stamping my foot to life, I shut the door.

I move swiftly now through every room of

Michael's house, opening and closing doors, snapping lights on and off. The rooms are smaller than you think back here. I note in passing an intense disorder. Unmade beds in two rooms. I move on. It is not until I come to the end of the corridor that I know he must be in the music room.

I don't switch on the light. He is sitting on the couch under the window. I go across to him.

He says: 'It's worse when it rains. It's like the whole planet's poisoned.'

Back in the house a phone starts ringing. Lauren? My mother? It doesn't matter. I am moving quite by instinct now.

(From *Sister Ships*, short fiction, 1986.)

LESLEY CORBETT
RIVER FEVER

The eleven years I lived in the Kimberley were some of the most vivid of my life, not only because I fell in love and had my children there, but because something deep within me was nourished in a way that it hadn't been since leaving Zimbabwe. There is a brooding power in the African countries I grew up in, an almost palpable presence pulsing through the bush and beating out from the plains and rocks. I had not felt it again until I came to Derby to work for the Kimberley Land Council, but there it was, that same power emanating from the land, seeming to call to me, so that something within me unfurled and came alive. Some evenings I would leave the Land Council office and walk out on to the mudflats, listening to the birds calling down the night as the air slowly cooled. It was particularly beautiful up past the cemetery where boab trees stood in silhouette against the darkening sky. If I was lucky I might catch the heavy flight of a coucal moving between the bloodwoods and bauhinias, and oh how it lifted my spirits in those difficult days when the drilling rig was heading for Noonkanbah.

One day I discovered the river, and ever since I have had river fever. Nothing gladdens me more than to stand beside a waterhole on some quiet stretch of the Fitzroy and listen to the call of black cockatoos, the cracked laughter of kookaburras, the high haunting whistle of kite hawks. In such places a stillness steals over me, and I am filled with such wonder and contentment, it's as if I am witnessing the heartbeat of the world.

The man I fell in love with lived in Fitzroy Crossing, two hundred and sixty kilometres away. Most weekends one of us made the journey. Usually it was Steve, puttering along in his little Suzuki, still dusty from travelling the dirt roads to Noonkanbah where he was helping the community try to prevent mining on sacred land. One Saturday during the wet season it was my turn to do the drive. It had been raining heavily for days, and about halfway to Fitzroy Crossing I came to a long stretch of flooded road. I got out and tested the water that in some parts came up to my knees. For a while I stood in the midst of that vast plain and simply listened. It was utterly silent, no other vehicle for miles. There was the quiet ripple of water, a faint sighing of the wind in the grass, and now and then a bird piping liquid notes into the air. After a while a semitrailer came along, and the driver leaned out his window and greeted me. When I told him I'd never driven through water that deep before, he suggested I follow him through. We moved in slow stately procession through the floodway, then I continued on, in a hurry now to see my fella.

The Fitzroy River wound through our lives. For a while Steve and I lived on its banks in a caravan. We got flooded out that year, the river rising higher than people had ever seen. At night we heard the terrible cries of cattle being swept downstream. Each morning Steve put a stick at the edge of the floodwaters, and each day they crept closer, until finally they engulfed our van, forcing us to take shelter with some friends.

As the river rose and spread across the landscape it became clear why Fitzroy Crossing was built in a series of scattered settlements. The town had fractured into islands of high ground separated by long stretches of muddy water. To get from one area to another you either waded, if it wasn't too deep, or you found someone with a boat. Snakes, spiders and goannas clung to the tops of submerged trees, while cattle bellowed mournfully, stranded on little patches of disappearing land.

By now the entire town was cut off. Great chunks had been eaten out of the bridge across Brooking Channel, and Plum Plain was under water. Road trains couldn't get through from Perth or Darwin, and supplies had to be brought in by air.

At the height of the floods we walked down to the main bridge and watched the river thundering down. It was an awesome sight, a mighty untamed creature filled with power that seemed intent on drowning all the land. Tragically some old people in one of the outlying communities lost their lives in the floodwaters when their boat overturned.

Fitzroy Crossing's water supply had become contaminated, and all across town people were falling ill with dysentery. Steve was one of them. For days he curled up at our friend's house, miserably clutching his stomach, and so when the floodwaters finally receded, the kindy teacher helped me clean the mud out of the van.

Our first child was conceived while we were living on the banks of the river. As my belly swelled into glorious new lines we decided not to risk being flooded out again. Housing was impossible to find in Fitzroy, so we moved to the tiny settlement of Camballin, with the river only a short drive away. Every chance we could we went fishing and swimming there, until the wet season set in and the road became impassable except to four-wheel drives. Amidst the tic tic of cicadas the spear-grass grew tall, and the plains turned a luminous green. Storm clouds swelled on the horizon, and our skin had a perpetual sweaty sheen.

Late one afternoon as sun tipped the spinifex with gold, I walked across the plain towards the Looma hills, feeling the pulse of the land and the powers slumbering within it. For a long time I stood there, calling out to the spirits of the land, asking them to protect the precious child I carried.

He was born early in February. By then floodwaters had crept over some of the roads around Camballin, and were lapping at several houses, but the main road remained open. When my waters broke we had to drive thirty kilometres along a corrugated dirt road, then another eighty kilometres of bitumen to reach Derby, the nearest town. We needn't have hurried. It was eighteen hours before he arrived and transformed our lives.

When we came home, we took him down to the river and dipped his feet in it, a kind of baptism, letting the water sing its way into his veins. We did the same with our second child. We were living back in Fitzroy Crossing when I became pregnant with him, and this time it was to Donkey Crossing I went, begging the river spirits to protect the little one nestled within me.

Not long after our second son was born we moved into a house of our own on a bush block near Derby filled with ghost gums, boabs, and bauhinias. It was a beautiful place to live, watching the seasons change and the clouds roll in. When the rains came we would dance out in them, and afterwards the kids would splash in the muddy pools and hurl mud at each other, the red becoming impregnated in their clothes. Sometimes we drove to Willare Bridge and watched the river rise, the boys delighting in flinging themselves into the gentler side currents and letting themselves be swept along. The best times though were during the dry season when we returned to our old haunts along the river. We would drive home in the dark, keeping a watchful eye out for cattle, still tasting the bream and cherrabun we had cooked over a fire. The slow murmuring song of the river ran through our dreams, calling us to return again and again.

I grew up with the seasons arranged the way they are in the Kimberley, where the rains fall during the time of greatest heat. Something elemental rebels in me when the seasons are reversed as they are in Perth, where rain falls cold and bleak through the long winter months, and never invites you to dance in it. I doubt I'll ever get used to it. Leaving the Kimberley was agony. Driving away from our house, my heart was crying out, begging me not to do this. A dull despair entered me as we turned south off the Broome Highway.

We live now on a bush block in the Perth hills with a winter creek filled with frog-song, but for years I mourned the Kimberley and felt hopelessly uprooted. In time I grew more contented, and learned to accept that there will always be this hollow place within me, this spirit longing. If I don't dwell on it, it dies down to a faint whimper rather than a roar that drowns out my life.

I went back a few years ago, flying into the arms of that beloved country, shedding tears of joy at sight of the first boab tree, my first glimpse of the river. As I lay beside my man that night in the glow of the campfire, the bright Kimberley stars reflected in the water, I was the richest woman on earth.

(From *Kimberley Stories*, an anthology, 2012.)

CONTRIBUTORS' NOTES

LIZ BYRSKI is a writer and former journalist with more than forty years experience in the British and Australian media. She is the author of seven novels, the latest of which is *In the Company of Strangers*, and eleven non-fiction books. Liz has been a broadcaster with ABC Radio in Perth, and an advisor to a minister in the Western Australian state government. She has a PhD from Curtin University, where she lectures in Professional and Creative Writing.

LESLEY CORBETT was born in Zimbabwe and immigrated to Australia in 1974, spending many years living in the Kimberley before moving to the hills outside Perth with her partner Steve Hawke and their two sons. In 1993 Fremantle Arts Centre Press published her children's picture book *Poor Fella*. A short story, 'A Change in the Weather', was published in the anthology *Summer Shorts 2*

(Fremantle Arts Centre Press, 1994). Other published short stories are 'The Last Frontier' (*Northern Perspective* vol. 15, 1992), and 'Old Yellow' (*Northern Perspective* vol. 17, 1994). 'River Fever' was published in the anthology *Kimberley Stories* (Fremantle Press, 2012).

A.B. FACEY was born in 1894 and grew up on the Kalgoorlie Goldfields and in the Wheatbelt of Western Australia. He went out to work when he was eight years old, and was droving in the North-West at fourteen. He had no formal education and originally wrote his acclaimed autobiography, *A Fortunate Life*, for his family. A.B. Facey died in 1982.

TRACY FARR grew up in Perth, Western Australia, but since 1996 has lived in Wellington, New Zealand. Her short fiction has been published in anthologies, literary journals and popular magazines, broadcast on Radio New Zealand, and been commended and shortlisted for awards in Australia and New Zealand. *The Life and Loves of Lena Gaunt* is her first novel.

ELIZABETH JOLLEY was born in the industrial Midlands of England and came to Western Australia in 1959 with her husband. She published twenty-three books, including novels, short fiction, poetry, nonfiction and plays. Celebrated as one of Australia's major writers, she also established a formidable international reputation, with her books being widely published throughout the world. She received an Order of Australia for services to Australian literature and was awarded honorary doctorates from four universities. She died in February 2007.

IRIS LAVELL has degrees in English, Psychology, and Theatre and Drama Studies, a teaching qualification, and a PhD in English and Comparative Literature. She has written four one-act plays, and as an actor performed in more than forty plays. Her poems have been published in the anthologies *Thirst* and *An Alphabetic Amulet*. Iris has worked for many years as a psychologist. *Elsewhere in Success* is her first novel.

NATASHA LESTER'S debut novel *What is Left Over, After* won the T.A.G. Hungerford Award for Fiction. Her short stories and poems have been published in collections including *The Kid on the Karaoke Stage*, and in journals such as *Wet Ink* and *Overland*. Natasha's latest novel is *If I Should Lose You*. She divides her time between writing novels, raising three children and teaching creative writing.

JOAN LONDON'S first book of short stories, *Sister Ships*, won the *Age* Book of the Year Award. Her second collection, *Letter to Constantine*, won the Steele Rudd Award and the WA Premier's Book Award for Fiction. Both were published by Fremantle Arts Centre Press. Her two novels, *Gilgamesh* and *The Good Parents*, both won national awards.

CHRIS MCLEOD is the author of three novels, *Man of Water*, *City of Skies* and *River of Snake*, and two collections of short fiction, *The Crying Room* and *Homing*. His work has appeared in Australian and international literary journals and has been recognised in awards including the International IMPAC Dublin Literary Award and the WA Premier's Book Awards. He is a former fiction editor of *Westerly*.

ADAM MORRIS is the author of *My Dog Gave Me the Clap* and an award-winning singer-songwriter as both a solo musician and with his musical outfit the Murder Mouse Blues Band.

MARCELLA POLAIN'S novel, *The Edge of the World* (Fremantle Press, 2007), was shortlisted for a Commonwealth Writers' Prize, and continues to be translated and published internationally. Her third poetry collection, *Therapy like Fish: new and selected poems* (John Leonard Press, 2008) was shortlisted for the Judith Wright Prize. Her short fiction has twice won the Patricia Hackett Prize, and her poems have been published in Europe, USA and the Middle East. She teaches Writing at Edith Cowan University and is working on a second novel.

CRAIG SILVEY grew up on an orchard in Dwellingup, Western Australia. His first novel, *Rhubarb* (2004), won Silvey the Best Young Australian Novelist Award from the *Sydney Morning*

Herald. His second novel, *Jasper Jones* (2008), has won numerous awards and was shortlisted in the Miles Franklin Literary Award and the International IMPAC Dublin Literary Award. Silvey is also the author of a picture book, *The World According to Warren*, with Sonia Martinez (2007). He lives in Fremantle, Western Australia.

ANNABEL SMITH'S first novel, *A New Map of the Universe*, was published by UWA Publishing in 2005 and shortlisted for the WA Premier's Book Awards. Her second novel, *Whisky Charlie Foxtrot*, was published by Fremantle Press in 2012. Annabel has been a writer-in-residence at Katharine Susannah Prichard Writers Centre and holds a PhD in Writing from Edith Cowan University.

JACQUELINE WRIGHT worked for many years as a teacher and linguist in the Pilbara and Kimberley on Indigenous Australian Aboriginal language, interpreting and cultural programs. Today she works as editorial associate at Magabala Books and sports producer at ABC Radio, Broome. She completed a Creative Arts Doctorate at Curtin University, where she is now an Adjunct Fellow. Her debut novel, *Red Dirt Talking*, won the T.A.G. Hungerford Award (2010) and was longlisted for the Miles Franklin Literary Award (2013) and the Dobbie Literary Award (2013).

MORE GREAT READS FROM
THE AUTHORS IN THIS BOOK

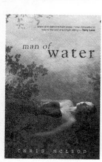